The man s...... .... me represented an irreplaceable element of strength, power, and efficiency that was ready to destroy the world.

He looked up at me and said, "You will begin the process of full disarmament and the establishment through the United Nations of a world government, or we will set it off. All of it. And there won't be anything but ash here for a hundred years."

They had gotten control of the reactors at Oak Ridge, Park Intervale, and a hundred other places in a coup. They had already set one off at Bismarck, North Dakota.

We had one day to meet their demands or they would begin to set the rest of the atomic devices off at a rate of one a day until we did ... or until there was nothing left.

WRITE FOR OUR FREE CATALOG

If there is a Pinnacle Book you want but can't
find locally, it is available from us—simply
send the title and price plus 25¢ to cover
mailing and handling costs to:

PINNACLE BOOKS
One Century Plaza
2029 Century Park East
Los Angeles, Ca. 90067

___Check here if you want to receive our
catalog regularly.

___Check here if you wish to know when the
next_____will be published.

THE
LAST TRANSACTION
Barry N. Malzberg

PINNACLE BOOKS   LOS ANGELES

THE LAST TRANSACTION

Copyright © 1977 by Barry Malzberg

All rights reserved, including the right to reproduce this book or portions thereof in any form.

An original Pinnacle Books edition, published for the first time anywhere.

ISBN: 0-52340-174-4

First printing, November 1977

Cover illustration by Ron Wilotsky

Printed in the United States of America

PINNACLE BOOKS, INC.
One Century Plaza
2029 Century Park East
Los Angeles, California 90067

For Nathaniel Wisch, M.D.
and for Roger Elwood

THE
LAST
TRANSACTION

PROLOGUE

WILLIAM ERIC SPRINGER: b. Pine Oaks, Illinois
7/4/10; educated in local public schools; B.S.,
University of Illinois 1932; LL.B., University of
Virginia 1935; practiced law in Virginia, Ken-
tucky, and Illinois 1935–40; Illinois State Legis-
lature 1940; assistant minority leader 1944;
elected Congress 1948; elected Senate 1950; majority whip 1954; reelected Senate 1956; majority
leader 1960; reelected 1962, 1968, 1974. Elected
president of the U.S. 1980; renominated and de-
feated 1984.

PERSONAL DATA: Married Eunice Con-
stance Blake, 1938; Arthur Blake Springer b.
1940 (d. 1963). Married Hope Johnson 1958 (d.
1987). Author, *Years of Decision, Years of Hope*
(1959); *The Power and the Vision, Memoirs of a
President* (1987). Autobiography in progress.
Residence: 1185 Park Avenue, NYC.

Don't think I can get a thing out today.

Not a thing, not a thing. Sensation of dim blockage not only of the mind but of the bowels; it is, then—and let me try to get this right—as if all of this rhetoric were choked within coils of possibility: too weak, distracted, dispirited even for simple recitation of the facts. Tomorrow, then, or perhaps the day after—the constant flickering of the light on this machine as I speak is a pain in the ass. Voice as light; the reduction of words to image. Incontinence beckons again.

Coming into Peoria there was music, five of the bands massed to greet me at the steps of the town hall, noise all around, color, return of native son in triumph after all these years. It must have hit me for the first time then—although again there might have been hints before then—a complete hint of disassociation. I did not know where I was. Suddenly all of it was flicking in and out of focus: one moment the town hall, the limousine, the noise, and the pressure against me on the seat (I thought, as I had a thousand times in open limousines, of Kennedy, leaning forward slightly to touch my shoetops with a glistening forefinger, which trembled only slightly out of the field of vision); and the next some dim, gray, open space in which I floated like a bottle bobbing in the sea, a *flick!* in the recession of consciousness—and then back into focus again, one high-school youth bleating madly through his sousaphone, dangling like an elevated prick into the car. But although I saw, I did not know where I was, literally could not place the segment for an instant: who was I? where was this? what was going on? And the panic began. Never had this hit me in public before. A few times perhaps in bed, once in a cabinet meeting—but those were moments instantly controlled. But this one went on, appallingly on. I could feel the sweat begin to come out of me in little ball-joints of excrescence, and I straightened, leaned against the seat, and opened my mouth, warning myself to take slow breaths. Slow breaths. Hope: "Bill, what is wrong? What's the matter, Bill?" Never could get a thing past that bitch—not that her knowledge ever did her any good either. "Bill, you're very white. Are you all right, Bill? All right?" shoving hip to thigh against me in the enclosure of the limousine then, and I could feel myself swinging perilously into alignment finally, a sense of history returning along with time and place, and I said, "Yes, Hope, I'm all right, everything is all right," forcing a trembling little wave above the door, the wind glancing off my palm, then another, and indeed I did feel better. Somewhere between the bleats of sousaphone and Hope's own kind, blurred words, I could feel assertiveness returning, a sensation that I had

4

made some awful passage and was now coming out through the other end—all illusory perhaps but very comforting at the time. There is nothing like going briefly crazy and coming away from it to give you a shot of optimism, let me tell you. Let me tell you that, among other things. We welcome the president of the United States. Returned native son for the first time in so and so many years. Triumphant reelection campaign. First Lady too. She pressed my palm, gave me little glances dappled by the sun. You might have thought—even the local dignitaries and Secret Service might have thought—that we were lovers. Ah, well. Future of America within our grasp. Future of Americans also within our grasp. The end of the century approaching, crucial choices for the next two thousand years—the next *four thousand* years—and then, just as I was coming toward the end of it, one more image of Kennedy thrust into mind as if seen through rips in the mesh of consciousness, and falling, falling into her arms, their arms, the burning of the brain. . . .

That was a very difficult election.

Eggs with bacon on toast with a side order of hashed browns. Sounds of the road rising and filtering through all the sounds of the diner. A 1938 Packard Eight, straight cylinders with floorshift and high cushions. Explosion of sun against the visors, the road falling.

Merrick is on duty during the days this week. He and Henry alternate, of course (I am very cunning and alert to everything that is going around me; this senility and now incontinence are merely by-products of my cunning; like the observant freak at the sideshow they permit me to watch the others without drawing attention to myself) so that Henry was my day-attendant last week and will again be next. But on the other hand, Merrick is the one with whom I have to contend *this* week, and I do not like him very much, although under all of the difficult circumstances attending this case, there is no particular reason why I should. Merrick is forty, or perhaps he is forty-two years old; he looks like a cabinet minister, at least in certain flashes and aspects of the light, but he is little more than a skilled male nurse—which is not to say that he is to be derogated on these grounds alone. I wonder why they will not allow me female nurses—but it is not mine to speculate. Perhaps they feel that I am at least potentially violent, but except for that one unfortunate situation, I have never been. Violent.

Tapes jamming in the recorder, the spool slamming to halt, and the tape exploding then in a filthy mess out of the machine and on the rug. It was necessary for me to call Merrick for assistance, my own old hands being insufficient to scoop the damned tape from the rug, untangle and feed it into the machine again. And in fury I

6

bellowed for Merrick, helpless tears coming into my helpless old eyes, my helpless old frame shuddering and shaking in its chair, the microphone falling away from my lips as I bellowed and bellowed for him . . . increasingly, I disgust myself. Self-revulsion may be the last identity of the aged, the last expression of the will which they are permitted. Merrick came in (I imagine that he is sitting in the outer room reading a newspaper, although this is pure sentiment; Merrick, I am convinced, can neither read nor write, undoubtedly he listens to my ravings with a disinterested ear, pausing now and then to take small, careful swallows from the pint bottle of gin which I can see bulging in his pocket) and saw the mess and stooped over to pick it up, shaking his head, his face carefully blank.

"Now, Mr. President," he said, "this is happening too often. This is the third time this week you've had an accident with the recorder, Mr. President. Don't you think that maybe you should rest for a while? Or at least you could use casettes, now casettes don't spill all over—"

"I'll do whatever I want," I said. Merrick does not bring out the best in me. "I don't want a cassette. I want something that I can feel. I want to see accumulation. Don't call me Mr. President."

"Why, Mr. President, you are the president, I mean you were. It's only proper—"

"Don't give me any of your shit," I said. Sometimes I enjoy using obscenity before Merrick merely to gauge his reaction. Henry never shrugs, is as likely to answer me scatologically as not, but Merrick underneath his shell of white has some lurking beast of Protestant ethic: obscenity disturbs him, even more when it comes from an ex-

7

chief of state. "Clean up that filthy mess and go," I said.

He continued at his work, casting shy, careful glances over his shoulder. "All of the excitement," he said, "all of this excitement is not so good for you, Mr. President. Perhaps a nap—"

"I don't want a nap," I said. "I don't want to be told what to do. I don't have to take orders from you. Don't call me Mr. President."

A sudden roiling dust came up before my eyes; I realized that I was about to incur another spell of weakness. Not two hours before the machine, not three hours out of the bed, and I felt myself beginning to lurch and totter once more inside, all powers failing. I could not bear for him to see my disgrace. "Get out of here, Merrick," I said.

He stood there, strips of tape like ribbons of state filtering through his fingers, one spool dangling from his wrist like a scrotal sac. His eyes showed new alertness. "You're not well," he said.

"Get out of here."

"Upsy-daisy, Mr. President," Merrick said, laying the spools and tape carefully on the floor and coming over to extend an arm, pull me crumpling from the chair. "Now, we'll just take care of that later. We'll just clean that up a little later on this morning and have it nice for you when you're ready to come back. We'll have everything for you later. But it's time for a rest now; you don't look well. And also, some medicine will make you feel much better."

I could not resist him. Falling across him, riding his back like an insect, I could see the layers of white rising against my eyes, a field of white, becoming all perception. I struggled

8

against him, flapped my hands like paper on the surfaces, but no good, no good. He carried me easily. He is 270 pounds. He used to be an amateur boxing champion, he once told me. There is no way in which I could resist him—and then again why should I? Without his presence, without the presence of the others in these rooms, how could I live? I would not trust myself to breathe.

"Come along, Mr. President," Merrick said, and we tottered and tumbled from the room. As we did this, I had a sudden jagged vision of the procession through the halls for the State of the Union and said to Merrick, "Yes, Mr. Speaker, yes," but he did not gauge the sense of this, having neither irony nor recollection, and after a time I did not gauge the sense of it either, being preoccupied with more immediate necessities. How can I continue the tapes if my health continues to flag? How will I finish my work?

Hovering above Eunice, Arthur's squalls from the next room mounting and mounting, it occurred to me that all I wanted to do was to finish, that lust or simple necessity had made me a beast and my concern was no longer for mutuality, for her pleasure, for the ethics of sex itself, but only to come and be done with it before the wretched screams became insuperable and she would have to rear from the bed, throw over the sheets, lumber off, sighing, into the next room to feed him. At the beginning I had performed with gentleness

9

and fire, just as she had asked, but as the first blade of sound came from his bedroom, the rhythm of my purpose broke and I was suspended on flaming wire, merely trying to come into her before all of it was gone and once again I would have to dwindle into the gloom of self, ponder my losses while listening to the slobbering and sucks from the next room. Completely supplanted. Jabbing and jabbing away at her, all purpose concentrated into my organ, I thought for an instant that I could break through into the other side of her, force her to an excess of feeling that she had not known before. But then it all went away, and I was in the capitol with the two of them, the governor looking at me grimly, his eyes slanting toward knowledge, then away in contrived disinterest in that way of his, and I told him, "You haven't got the votes. That's all. They're not there."

"You're job isn't to tell me I don't have the votes," he said. "Your job is to get me the votes."

"We can't," Connors said, looking away from me. "We've been up and down the aisles on this one. The resistance is too strong; they're getting too much pressure downstate. It won't go through."

"Yes it will," the governor said. He jabbed Connors once in the chest, not too lightly, and reinforced that conviction which I had had from the first—that there was in the governor perhaps the desire to possess, but in Connors it was the need for possession, and this was the real, the operable relationship, Connors' pervasive need to be fucked, to literally be empty and dominated and overtaken. By that insight I turned away—it was too disgusting—and found myself in fact

10

walking out of the office, and the governor said, "Bill, where the fuck are you going?"

"I'm going away," I said. "I have nothing else to say. There's nothing more to do here. We came to give you a message and now it's given. We haven't got the votes."

"Stay here," the governor said. "I want to talk—"

"No," I said. I do not know where that sudden conviction came from, but it came flaring from within; and it was as if I was seeing Connors, the governor himself through the other end of a very powerful telescope, dwindled figures revolving in statuary configuration like ruined stars whose light reflected the disasters of a hundred million years ago. "I can't stay and I can't talk. You say you're asking for information, but you're really not. You say you're here to listen, but you're only interested in telling. I can't go through with it anymore. Not under those terms."

"Come on, Bill," Connors said. There was a little wavering edge in his voice—or then again I may have merely constructed this out of my own disordered perceptions. "You can't walk away from this. We've all got to stay and figure—"

"No," I said again and opened the large door, shoving at it, pushing, grunting a little. "I won't stay. I won't participate in this anymore. You can't ram this through because they're on your ass, and if we try to, it's going to drag down all of us, including myself, and I won't have that— I'll take gas or something I've made up myself. But I'll make damned sure that it's mine and that it's worth the trouble and that a lot of people see me taking the pipe so that they'll remember what I did for them."

11

This statement simply came out of me. In retrospect it may have to be recorded as one of the Great Moments of Political Insight—in fact, I trust that it will be. But moments of great insight never look like that at the time, all that they seem to be is a particularly appropriate response to a particularly grating stimulus.

"I mean that," I said, and even as Connors bellowed and whined behind me, the governor grumbling quietly, as was his habit, I walked out of the doors and through the padded surfaces of the statehouse, shaking my head. "Excuse me, excuse me," to servants, porters, legislative scribes, housekeepers, and so on, "I'll find my own way out."

In retrospect, it can be seen that I did indeed find my own way out, but at the time it was simply obvious to me that the Public Service Commissioner was a crook and was taking kickbacks from power and light—and anyone over the age of twelve with a passing glance at the newsstands could see this—so why get involved? And even if the commissioner was not a crook, even if he had been hung in the newspapers, as they say, well, the shadow is as good as the act, sometimes better in this trade, and what to say?

I felt my seed rising within me, little kernels shaking and shaking in the dim interior of myself, crying for issuance with their little separate voices, while far below me Eunice twirled and grunted on the spit of myself, her eyes closed, her fists coiled, her breasts seeming to shrivel and retract within. She was a good-hearted woman, had her points, never tried to take them away from her, but she retreated from sex, found it a descent rather than a rising. I do not believe that

12

in the twelve years we had together I was able to
bring her to orgasm more than once or twice—
and those were accidents.

"Get it over with," she was saying, the screams
pouring heavily from the next room, "for God's
sake get it over with!" Not a pretty attitude, one
must admit, from one's own wedded wife, but on
the other hand that was my desire too, that was
all that I was interested in doing—getting it over
with. And finally, with squeals and small cries, I
felt myself shuddering, beginning to move toward
the edge—over which (I always had this fantasy)
I might tumble fecklessly and never be heard
from again—reaching forward, grasping her
breasts, pulling out the nipples and two small
stains of milk opening, and beginning to spread
out from their flat, slippery surfaces as I poured
into her.

"Well, are you done now?" she said, still sliding
in and working her fissure. "Is it over?" Her eyes
wide and moist, no intent to hurt there, I could
see that, nor intent to insult; she simply did not
know what was happening. At length I came off
her in little, lofting stages, sliding first to belly,
then flat to chest, and coming off her in a grumbling turn that sent my eyes ceilingward. "All
right," she said, standing, taking her nightgown
from the bottom of the bed, patting it into place
around her, "all right, then," heading through the
door. And I lay there, soaked by own own semen
and the cries of my first-born, looking at the patterns which the cobwebs made on the ceiling—or
maybe the spirals and network were merely in my
eyes, filmed against the pupils, those cross-hatches
through which I would have to perceive all of my

13

life as I would know it, endless imperfection, perfect patterning.

Connors died of a heart attack on the floor six months after that while making a quorum call.

Going down to Joliet, the three of us in Mack's La Salle, beating off in the back seat early because (we were told) it would make us come slower with the whores, and Mack saying, "Nate Leopold went to this place, they still talk about him there." That was a shock, going to the whorehouse where Nate Leopold had been; for a moment, even in the midst of the pictures I was making in my head, a clear, bright image of the dead boy's eyes, staring—was there any collaboration between Babe and myself? Was anything welding us together other than the simple, sodden need to fuck, and at the same whorehouse?

"What the fuck does that matter?" Jim was saying beside me, "Everybody goes here, even he would, but I don't think he ever got it off." That was something to think about also.

"How about Loeb?" I asked them. "Did he ever go here too?" And they began to laugh. I could not quite understand the laughter for a moment, with the La Salle slamming along the state highway, hitting the rocks, making the curves perilously—and then at last I got it, could see the joke too.

"Oh," I said, "oh, I see—they could have saved the money, helped each other out." And that was it, Mack laughing and slamming the gearshift, Jim hitting me on the knee, thinking of the whores and their moist temples into which I would evacuate—then a long, singing blank space and into the whorehouse itself, a two-family on a sidestreet and slamming at last against the girl on the bed, her body long, my prick long, the two of us melding densely, surprising response from her, considering that she was a prostitute. But then again most of what I knew about them I knew only from books—there were many years before I understood that passion had to do with situation, not so much with role. And then at last, falling away from her, breathing pause on the bed, I asked, "Did Nate Leopold ever come in here?" and—oh, my God, the look on her face— oh, my Good Lord, how she looked at me. Then (I am beginning to drool into the microphone) she *hit* me—slobber all over the mike, my hands palsied and freckled, shaking against the wire, the spools overflowing, starting to foul again. Do not go gentle, my friends.

Inauguration: they needed something simple and straightforward, something at last which would cut through all that had happened and make sense of it for them. This is the key to political success, Henry, do not kid yourself. Are you listening, Henry? Of course you're not listening, sitting over there in the corner reading a newspaper, while I sputter and babble into this machine. *Henry*, you'd do far better listening to me than chasing those lies . . . ah fuck yourself, you asshole, you want to read the newspaper, it's all right with me—just make sure that the urinal is strapped tight onto the leg, eh, Henry? No piss into your careful cupped palm for you.

Something simple and to the point, which would tell where we had been and where we were going, not that anyone knew where the fuck we had been—of course not—that anyone knew where we were going to go or why or for that matter there was any need to go *anywhere*, the need to go places having been deeply ingrained into the American psyche long before Springer, Bill Eric, first saw the mild continental light—but what is there to say? Ours not to reason why, Henry, ours merely to carry on the traditions of our fore-fathers. And so in this two hundred and fourth year of the republic, in this ninety and sixth year before the tricentennial, Springer, Bill Eric, en-deavored to add his voice to all those who had preceded, beckoning all those who would follow.

No need to evoke images of the bicentennial, of course. That was better not discussed. No, this was a looking forward, not a looking back, solder-ing old enemies together, slaking old passions; and so it was resolved to give them a little of this, a little of that, a little of progress, and a little of eternity, a soupcon of dedication, and an earnest nod of or to tradition . . . you know how it is, Henry. And so the speech grew and grew through the sheer and shaping hands of the assembled team; and at last, in the cold and blue weather of that Washington January (it was decided to keep the ceremonies in Washington, after all; it was important for morale, to keep up appearances;

surely you recall all of that, Henry?), Springer, Bill Eric, was inaugurated as the thirty-*ninth* president of the United States. Do you recall that? Standing here in the place where others have stood, we pick up the standard which has fallen, countless times been raised, countless times knowing that in America this is the way it must always be and we are framed eternally between what we can and can never do . . . but what we can never do today we will do tomorrow. Pick up the standard, let fall the standard, possibilities and promise, the awesome splendor of this great land as riven through its landscapes . . . ah, well, compromise candidates arising from bitter national conventions must do the best they can. It is not to say how it might have been but only how much worse all could be spoken. Rhetoric will get you nowhere, Henry.

And then the Inaugural Ball, splendid procession of choices, seven of them in seven neighborhoods with seventeen hundred guests at each . . . seventeen hundred times seven to welcome the advent of the compromise choice. A bow here, nod there, dance at every one, and Hope beside me talking, talking, eternally talking; there was no end to the woman, no end to shutting her up, even then she must have been senile, although I put the best face on the matter that I could and simply tried to keep her under wraps as much as possible, her voice ringing the changes through the night, her gestures spasms as she danced, as she waved . . . the seven dances with her were horrors, particularly the last, where she lurched to a stop, and then simply fell, collapsed to the floor, her face constricted in that deathhead clown's mask which she had had for years. I cannot tell you for how long I had been seeing her face in only that aspect, all of the passion which I had felt for her parodied, inverted by the gross, coarse, and cruel lines of that face; but still in certain slashes and dashes of light, it was possible for me to think of her as attractive, if only as a perversion. But this last time, as she went sliding over, frantic pelting from the floor, and then the guards hauling her to her feet, leading her away, circling her protectively as I followed, all of us then swarmed over by the larger number of guards and into the limousine itself, Hope panting, wiping streaks from her forehead with a handkerchief in a gesture curiously masculine (I had never known a woman to wipe her forehead in just that way until I met Hope and saw her do it and considered it initially attractive; well, I learned better), and then whisked into the limousine into the night behind the stolid shoulders of the driver (I never knew their names, not once, not ever), turning to Hope then, I said, "There was no need for that, there was no need for that, Hope. You're fifty-seven years old."

"You old fool," she said, "you old fool, you're seventy."

And do you know, Henry, do you know something? Not until that very moment had it occurred to me that I was seventy years old. I mean, it was known, chronology cannot be ignored—and there was the question of it to cover in the election by presenting a vigorous image and calling upon after years of violent decadent youth and its convulsions, wisdom and statesmanship and a firm older hand on the helm of government—but until that instant, age had been nothing more than an administrative problem, having nothing

18

doing with me in any personal sense or having to do either with the failing of powers. Looking at her then and seeing how her eyes caught mine, I realized for the first time that I was a very old man indeed. And the limousine, sheathed, sped through the night. What a bitch, Henry.

What a bitch.

"World government," he said to me, maybe he was twenty-five years old. This was the representative they had selected on their terms to visit me. An insult, but what could I do? What could any of us do? "World government, man, or we set off the piles."

I did not know what to say. Dolan in the corner twitched. "You filthy bastard," he said.

"Get him out of here," their representative said and twitched a finger at Dolan. "I don't care if he's the fucking secretary of state, I don't care if he's the fucking head of the Federal Bureau of Investigation, you get him out of here right now. This is man on man."

He was neither. He was the vice-president. It occurred to me that this man genuinely did not know who Dolan was and he did not care—that was the kind of people we were dealing with. "You'd better go, Harry," I said.

"And let that shit get away with this?" Dolan said, streaks on his forehead, a slam as he brought his palms together. He had been the governor of Nebraska, and a lousy one as far as I could gather (what do we know of the statehouses in the Senate? statehouses even our own, I mean). But he had the proper conservative appeal, and the polls showed that I ran better with no one than with anyone—and Dolan was as close to no one as we could get. "This is the president of the United States."

"Get him out, man," the representative said again. I never got his name. He never gave it. Of course, it would stand to reason that they have no names; what would they have needed names for? That meant identification, which was exactly what they did not need. Besides, they said, they were not individuals; they represented an irreplaceable element of strength, a group of power and efficiency where any individual could be replaced by any other. "Get that son of a bitch out."

"You bastard," Dolan said, standing, but I hit the buzzer on my desk and the service came in, and I said, "Get that man out of here!" pointing not to the representative, who they would have expected, but at Dolan. And before he could raise his arms to protest, the vice-president was being dragged out of the offices, the door closed, and I was alone again with the representative, without secretary or bodyguard. This was one of their conditions. "World government," he said again, looking at me, "we get a full field disarmament and the establishment through the United Nations of a world government, or we set it off. The whole thing. There won't be anything but ash here for a hundred billion years."

"You wouldn't do it," I said calmly, although of course they would do it—wasn't that precisely the point? They had gotten hold of the reactors at Oak Ridge and Park Intervale and a hundred

20

other places in a coup the magnitude of which I could not even understand, and their ability to detonate was established. They had already set off an underground at Bismarck, North Dakota, for demonstration purposes, they said, and were ready to unload under a silo at some location in Kansas. One a day they told us, one a day until we capitulated and agreed to a unilateral disarmament under the terms of a world government. They claimed that they were doing the same thing in Russia, in China, in Israel, in France—but we had no evidence of this. Of course, they made it clear that one of their preconditions was a concealment from all intelligence sources so that each nation would have to deal with the situation on its own. Wasn't that true? Were we telling anyone? The situation, as the representative said, was quite clear-cut. For the first time in forty years, an American president was confronted with a clear set of choices. For our sake, of course, he hoped that we would make the right decision.

He reminded me of Arthur. Did I tell you that already, Merrick? Merrick is in this room, looking at me with his usual mixture of gloom and apprehension; unlike Henry, he is not a reader but rather a starer; looking at those fixated, glistening eyes, it is possible to believe that Merrick is looking deeply into me, is seeing, as it were, my very soul . . . until I remind myself of the fact that neither Merrick nor Henry are of any capacity whatsoever; if they were, they would not be male nurses, day-shift, to a sniveling and senile ex-president locked up like a rat in the steaming, fuming quarters of his four-and-a-half-room prison on the eleventh floor of this very old-style residential building. Instead, Merrick and Henry would be out in the world writing instructions for injections and baths rather than merely administering them. They have satisfied the very minimum requirements of the board? Am I right, Merrick? Of course, the man is beyond taking offense; there is no way in which I could cause him to lose his temper, and if I did, it would merely result in his replacement. Merrick appreciates his position too much. There are only two living ex-presidents, and although one of them may be rightly considered to be as good as dead, the other one is not in the best of condition either. Merrick appreciates the honor and obligation of his position and would do nothing to sacrifice it. Isn't that right? Observe that stupid beam now, the slight lift of the eyebrows, that gleaming, steaming beam that both reveals and conceals feeling. You think that I'm a real son of a bitch, don't you, Merrick? I couldn't care less. I do not think well of you either. I think you are unequal to any challenge which I could pose. Stop staring—you're making me nervous now.

The man reminded me of Arthur. Stop staring; I might piss all over the floor, over this gleaming cuspidor locked in my thigh—and where would you be now? He was much younger than Arthur would be now, of course, and yet I could imagine Arthur, forty-four years old, wearing this outlandish garb, the highly stylized garb of what they called the resistance. I could even see that if Arthur had lived to this age—which he would have done and well beyond except for one tiny, genetic accident—he might have had this expression in his eyes, this bone of cynicism lanced through and just underlying the intentness of

22

that face, the cast of the eyes in their fanatic
glare undercut by the measured outlines of the
skull beneath, the skull that knew all, touched and
apprehended everything, and would soon enough
assume its primacy, the rest of the flesh tumbling
into corruption. Oh, yes, looking at this man I
might have been looking at Arthur, which is not
to say that I was looking at him, which is not to
say that my mind did not remain clear and alert
through all of this, uncluttered by noisome speculations and sentimental lurches toward my de-
ceased son, who it would be hard under the best
of circumstances to see as a victim. But then, that
one swinging glance past him to look out the
window toward the parade grounds, what I had
deliberately selected to give me inspiration (presidents, of course, can get away with anything, and
now and then they try) at the enormous cost of
shifting office quarters to the other side of the
wing, at the cost of getting illuminated floodlights
and one-way paneling in the window—and then
my gaze swinging back, I confronted him and
could see then that he was serious, that he was
absolutely serious, that he meant what he was
saying. And up until that moment, I think I had
been proceeding—all of us had been—on the
assumption that there was an element of parody
here, an element of outrage deliberately contrived
so that at the last moment they could whip away
the mask and laugh, having confronted us only
with our own fears . . . but no, no, and no again.
Looking at him I could see the strange, mooning
cast of the fanatic, below the level of the chin, the
tremble of the hands. "You have no time to think
about this," he said, "nor will we negotiate. You
are to give your response now."

"I don't know," I said. "I would have to discuss it with the cabinet. I would have to make a public statement of some sort. There is no way that what you want can be accomplished without—"

"Don't temporize, you fool," he said to the president of the United States. "We've lived with your rationalizations for forty years. We don't have to any more; we hold all the power. You must make your decision now. Dismantle or die."

"You don't understand," I said, "there are factors here that are beyond your comprehension, there are intricacies—"

"There are no intricacies. You merely create the idea of complexity to save your own skins, to maintain your totalitarian control. You resist change because change would undercut your own position, that's all. Well," he said, leaning forward, his eyes glazed with excitement, "it occurred to me that this was perhaps the key to any analysis of the situation." He was deeply excited, profoundly stirred—and why should he not have been? Under the circumstances, I would have been the same. "You must decide now. What will you do?"

And I sat there behind the desk in the East Wing, looking out at the parade grounds again, then back at him, swinging in vision, his luminescent face, the glowing of the grounds, before my reach the telephone with which I would communicate the orders; and there was no way to tell him, no way to tell him, Henry and Merrick, at all that he had misjudged the situation and that even if I were to use that telephone, it would make no difference. Dispersion. The fragmentation of power. There was no way in which I could do for him what he was asking, even if he had been Arthur

24

himself and the appeal had been a restoration to life, an end to the stinking and eternal corruption of his flesh.

I can take a walk if I want to, Merrick. I can do anything I want to do; get me my overcoat and my cane, get me my little walker and stand close behind me, and you and I will go out onto Park Avenue like a pair of patients etherized upon a table, just you and I, stumbling and staggering down the length of the Avenue . . . why, it would be a sensation—my first public appearance in what? two months? two years? It is difficult to recollect but certainly in a very long time anyway. And I think that I deserve to go out; it is high time that I took the air again. And you have no right to keep me prisoner in this apartment which, very cunningly, I know that you are doing. I know that you are merely representatives of interests in whose best judgment it would be a disaster if I were to see the street again, if I were consequently to be seen in public. Wild Bill. Wild Bill Springer. You are afraid of the walker, the cane, the overcoat, the cannister taped to the thigh, and the slight, deadly stain of drool which would come from one corner of my mouth as thee and me went strolling down the Avenue. That is what you mean.

But I say that I have a perfect right to take a walk if I wish; I say that no one is more entitled than Wild Bill to a stroll down the Park Avenue of his life and dreams. Remember old Harry Truman tapping his way down the Avenue in the sunset of his years, his cane cleaving out small, neat patterns on the concrete as he scurried ahead of the press and attendants in pursuit ... is it possible that I am obsessed by old Harry, that I am trying myself to reconstruct old Harry in some conceived valley of the self so that it is not Wild Bill so much as Independent Harry that will be rolling down the Avenue? I do not know about that, Merrick. We ex-presidents, of course, are a very small and select group, our devices and motives not to be understood by the run of men; I am entitled, after all, to take my referent from my peer group—wouldn't you say so, Merrick? Bring me my paraphernalia!

Of course, this is impossible; I˙ see it quite clearly now and you needn't stare at me in that way, Merrick. I am not at all stupid, despite the appurtenances of senility which you may observe in my psyche and on my person, my senility being carried around with me the way that a fat, elderly lady might tug on a suitcase chained to her and filled with her most necessary possessions; despite all of this, as you say, I am stimulatingly alert and cognizant of my situation, and the higher cerebral faculties remain clear and well preserved. I am extraordinarily lucid today, Merrick; even I can appreciate this lucidity, admit that there are not many mornings on which I share this balance of humor and insight ... so let me tell you why I cannot walk out upon the Avenue. Let me make perfectly clear to you in the words of another ex-president, as they say, why I cannot go out tap-tapping upon the concrete of the Avenue, followed by faithful attendants and admiring press, gather-

26

ing awe-stricken glances from passersby like flowers as I float down the avenue of the memory.

I am no fool, Merrick. My public appearance would be scandalous and embarrassing. I may not be the first president or ex-president to have fallen upon the appearances of senility, but I am the first to have done it at such an advanced age; and my appearance, as any fool can tell, is absolutely shocking. I can hardly believe myself on my occasional glances into reflective surfaces (all mirrors having been cunningly removed from these rooms), the extent of my deteroriation. It would be a demoralizing and terrible thing for me to appear in public, far better to keep me here on a high floor under cover of male nurses, the tape recorder for sustenance and company, bleating whines from the sounds of the reversed tape as I dictate my memoirs . . . oh yes, I am working on my memoirs. That, at least, has been made known to the public and explains my seclusion over the last two years. The need for absolute privacy as I dictate my memoirs, bring them into organized format, the story of the eighties, the administration of Bill Eric Springer. Although a healthy, hale, hearty, happy, hamstrung, and hellacious eighty years old, I have reached that stage of life where I realize that I must conserve my energies and turn inward if I am to make my last great contribution to the unborn generations of mankind. Of course, I can understand this and so can the press and my many admirers; it explains why no interviews can be given and why I have not been seen in public for so many years since that distressing incident of which we will not speak now. Perhaps later. Have I got it, Merrick? Do I understand the situation? You must have thought that I was a fool if you did not think I knew what was going on . . . but as I said, I feel extraordinarily lucid today, little slants of sunlight pouring through latticework, casting mysterious patterns on the floor, little filigrees and filaments of the Presidential Seal I would imagine in my not-too-disordered consciousness . . . oh, yes indeed, I feel today as if I could, if I really had to, control my situation.

Then too the death of my dear wife Hope, her sudden and unfortunate demise barely two years ago has turned me into something of a recluse. Everyone knows how much support and cheer I obtained from this devoted woman through the twenty-nine years of our marriage, how much of my late political career was the product of her guidance and patient counsel, how the bitch and I had a relationship which—magnified by our childlessness and the great and awful pressures of national polictics—had as many secrets as a child's closet. . . . Oh, yes indeed, the media have been very good on the question, standing aside respectfully at the funeral, honoring me more in the breach than the observance . . . one could hardly tell from my stone-cold composure at the very private funeral how deeply shaken I was, and since then, of course, I have never been the same . . . it is no small thing for a seventy-eight-year-old man to lose a devoted mate of twenty-nine years who was twenty years younger than he . . . ah, yes, that would bring the thrust of mortality.

So no excuses have to be made for my failure to dodder out to Park Avenue and take the sun. On the other hand, excuses *would* have to be made if I were to do so; the effect upon so many of my devoted friends and one-time supporters would be extensive, ah, most astonishing: They would hardly know what to make of it.

So I understand quite well, Merrick, why it is impossible for me to go outside. It has been almost two years since I have stirred from these rooms given me by a grateful government along with the lavish attendances of two orderlies, similarly provided for day service and a group of night servants who I never see, being promptly anesthetized into torpor at 6 p.m. every day by your merciful needle and attentions. . . . Really, gratitude oozes from every pore of me at this moment, so as others might be drenched by sweat so as I by gratitude . . . it is not necessary for you to look at me in that way, Merrick. I am perfectly in control, perfectly in control of myself.

We want a world government and complete dismantling of the piles, or we are going to detonate. Ah, yes. That was a reasonable attitude suitable for calm dialogue and discussion. The line could have been delivered by you, Merrick. I think that you would have done it with even a flatter affect.

Thinking of Kennedy, the astonishing mortality rate of U.S. presidents, not only the twenty-year curse (which gave me ample pause, you may be sure—oh, yes indeed, there was a reason why that was a good year for a compromise candidate) but the succeeding administrations, one wrecked by assassination, the next by near-assassination and repudiation, the third broken from within, the fourth spectacularly its own victim . . . oh, yes, it was hard to ride straight in cars. Often, unconsciously, I would find myself curled over in the car in a *crouch,* my head moving kneeward, my knees moving headward, balled into a fetal posture, anticipating some Enormous Shock which would explode like a line of tracer fire from temple through skull through consciousness . . . heaving over myself in the car until Hope, if she was with me, would tap me on the shoulder and say, "Bill, Bill, you've got to straighten up. Stop thinking, Bill." And I would turn toward her (always, always I would turn toward her) with that embarrassed smile and say, "Just thinking, just thinking," and she would say, "Bill, if we don't give them a good appearance, if we show fear, if we can't give them that appearance, then it's worse for them, worse for us," thinking as always of that place between the shadow and the act where all of the feeling began; and I would straighten up, guilty, mopping little beadlets of sweat from my brow, waving, waving until the urge to hunch over like some animal pulling threads in the viscera would come again and I would slump over to myself in the eave of the limousine, her own face impermeable in the light; she would give them nothing at all, not even at the end would she break—only that one time which came much later and had nothing to do with those rides.

Once, in Dayton, coming for a dedication of the Peace Center, someone took a shot at the car as we were coming out of it. It was strange, after living with the irreality, the conception of it for so many years, the actual occurrence seemed almost offhand, incidental; in fact, we did not know what had happened until we saw in the distance

30

local police dragging off a screaming man waving and flaunting something gleaming in his hand. Only then did I manage to juxtapose the spang of shot off the car door and the picture of the man to realize that what had happened was an assassination attempt. But something known in dreams and conception over and over again is never the same, absolutely never the same in reality—like sex, which is all flesh, tugging and pain in the activity while not being at all like that in the mind —so assassination would have been the same way.

It occurred to me then that it could have been in just that dull and unbelieving fashion with which the bullet could have struck home; lying on the stones and gravel, the blood running out of me, I would not have believed that what had happened could have occurred, because I had always conceived—even I, who should have known better —assassination as being an essentially glamorous business, something high about it, high and exalting, ringing epiphany as the shots struck the brain, a feeling of conclusion as one slumped toward one's wife or self in immolative glee . . . but no, it would not have been anything like that at all. It was always a man in an undershirt, a crowd that did not know what was going on, flesh against flesh, heat and stones, and scuffle and annoyance; that was all that it was ever going to be, the damned *corporeality* of it, like sex, was blood and flowing. Well, that was how assassination would be, and no glow to it at all, not even in retrospect; in retrospect it would simply be death and nothing else. But still, even with that insight bubbling and bobbing around in the waters of the mind like a troll behind a fishing boat, it was still necessary to go through all the acts of ceremony which had brought us there . . . the Peace Center, the steps, the library, the dedication, the speech exactly as laid out in the scheduling; only one corner of the mind exploded into lips mumbling and babbling to itself deep in the pocket of the brain about what had happened—but that never to reach outside, you can be sure. One must learn to be sealed off; one must do what one does without thought and on reflex, this being the key to politics and show biz. And certainly after thirty-five years, I was able to do so, miming the activities of interest while putting far into that corner of the brain that chewed and regurgitated death any considerations of what might have happened to me. Later, on the way to the airport, we got a report from the service: he had been taken to a police station . . . he had collapsed . . . he had been taken to a hospital . . . he was in serious condition . . . he had had a cerebral hemorrhage . . . he was under artificial life-sustaining means . . . he was an itinerant, a loner, a wanderer, an anonymous individual of no background . . . the life-support mechanisms would bring him around, hopefully . . . we might get the full story someday. . . . Even then I knew he was going to die. We would know nothing. We would never know anything.

"He is going to die," I said to Hope on the plane. "He is going to die; all of them die; and we will know nothing at all right up until the very end."

"I don't know what you're talking about," she said. "Can't you forget this?" her own face blank, impermeable; the woman would show nothing. It was not until much, much later that I understood that this was because, most likely, there was nothing to show. "Can't you put this out of your mind? It doesn't mean anything." And I said again, "He is going to die," but not even thinking of him now, rather my attention distending, moving outward past the wing of the plane to the unimaginable land outside, striations brown and green beneath the clouds, structures slashed out of the wild, empty spaces: America.

"I saw it coming for a long time," Eunice said. "I knew it was going to happen—do you think I'm a fool? I won't give you a divorce; I'll ruin your career." (Perhaps I am compressing all of this a bit, but this is a license one is permitted when trying to dictate one's memoirs under vast and increasing time pressure—I might stroke out anytime—and certainly this was the evolving sense of it.) "You want to run for president someday; you certainly want to be reelected; you can't do it with a nasty divorce. I'll fight you, Bill. I'll make it miserable for you."

"Don't be ridiculous," I said. "It hasn't been a marriage for ten years, Eunice, you know that, ever since Arthur—"

"Don't you talk about Arthur. I never want you to mention Arthur's name again, do you understand that? That's an obscenity to me—to hear you mention Arthur's name. You have no right to say it now, you get away from me, you go back to your Senate Office Building, you—"

"Eunice," I said, "don't be ridiculous," I said again, "I'm just telling you this as a courtesy. You know there's no marriage—we haven't even lived together for years. You can't claim that—"

"You disgust me," she said, "you are filth. You are obscene. All of you are obscene and all of you are filth, but you disgust me more than any of them because I have been too close to you and I know your lies. You will never get a divorce." She was old and ugly. Always she had been old and ugly to me, even when she was young; but now I could see this. "Get away," she said again.

"Eunice," I said, "I'm trying to do the right thing here. I'm trying to tell you the truth, but you won't listen. If you listen, it will do us both a world of good, Eunice. There's nothing painful about the truth—"

"You bastard," she said. She was always swearing at me; she would curse me all of the time. Her body was a curse, framed in the pattern of obscenity on the bed. And entering her, moving low toward her open spaces, was to puncture the *u* in *fuck*. I never felt anything other than dirty when I was screwing her, but this, I want to emphasize, has nothing to do with my reasons for leaving her; simple guilt or doom would not be sufficient to leave that woman, not ever. I would need something far more concrete, more viable, something which would function as an alternative. But this is going back a long long way, and it is not really possible to talk of my mental state at that time, thirty-four years ago.

"You bastard," she was saying, "I'll make it hell for you." But my mind was already spinning off in some vague direction apart from her, likewise my body. I could feel myself filled with abstraction; and looking at me then, she must have realized that her time was past, there was no way

34

that she could reach me, no way in which she could get through to me again—and this more than anything else is what must have broken her, caving her, kneeling into herself, her body a declension.

"Was it for nothing?" she said. "All of this then, was it for nothing?" And I wanted to say, "Eunice, you are getting upset over abstractions; Eunice, there are no issues here; Eunice, there is no concrete thing to which you can point and say this is what you will miss, this is what you will gain by not leaving me; there are no concretizations left in our marriage, everything is abstractions; we are fighting over abstractions; even this, my decision to leave you is an abstraction; I have decided to do it now, and I am telling you this at breakfast in the sunlit parlor of our five-room duplex, but then again I could have told you a year ago or two months from now in another parlor not floodlit as this one is; I could have done it at night in our bed or in the enclosure of a limousine ... Eunice why won't you be sensible? It isn't me you are reacting to here but something, someone else, someone who you do not even know, emotions which you are supposed to feel, not the reality of the situation but merely the felt reality."

Oh, this was some monologue that I had stored up for her—and who is to say that it would not have worked, that I would not have somehow punctured through into the center of her and yanked her by the force of my rhetoric to a new apprehension. But I said nothing else to her at all, merely turned, merely moved away from there; there was nothing else to say and I simply wanted to leave. ...

On our honeymoon, the first night in the New

Yorker Hotel in Manhattan, the bridegroom tense and white-faced, the bride impermeable in the blues and browns into which she had changed right after the ceremony, sitting with her hands folded in the airplane, her head leaning against my shoulder, a silent and closed-in amusement on her face; and then in the hotel in the room as I had moved toward her, she had said, raising her hand, "We'll do exactly what we are supposed to do, but first I'm going to get some dinner." Seven hours in the plane and I moved away from her— who is not to say that I was not as relieved as disquieted, the responsibility of the wedding night suddenly awesome, although this is not to say that there had not been substantial playing around before the marriage, particularly in the last week before the ceremony, when she wanted to do it desperately but I held off from banging her for what I termed were moral reasons, but probably were just fear.

Looking across her at the table between us in the coffee shop, that closed-in aspect still on her mouth, that dance of amusement in her eyes, and just touching knees under the table, then all the way back up in the elevator, I hardly knew her; into the bedroom and she into the bathroom first —I did not know her at all then—in a pink nightgown I had never seen before filled with ribbons; back to the bed, and I into the bathroom into my clumsy pajamas, then back into the room which was suddenly dark; finding her in the bed that way I did not know her at all, but I was sure that I loved her; love would make everything work out, that was how we felt in those days . . . and then leaning above her in the darkness, poised on an elbow, saying, "The bridegroom is absolutely terrified, you know." And something had reached out of her, some bird vaulting in the room, hammering its pressure into my chest, and she had brought me murmuring against her, talking into my ear, biting it, filling my ear with confidences and lashings of her tongue, and I had begun to rise, sputtering beneath her, until suddenly that which was shapeless and without form in the void was no longer shapeless but had every purpose under the heaven and cold. Cold, I dug my way into her, feeling her yielding slowly, moving up further toward her center, then, feeling one small pocket of resistance caving easily under me as I wedged my way upward, and it was almost too easy (but she had warned me; hadn't she warned me already of a childhood accident which had caused a rupture? and I had no reason to disbelieve her, no reason at all), digging further and further, and suddenly feeling was all around me. She was crying underneath me. I was crying in rhythm too, and inch by inch I felt consummation being yanked out of me in what was pain and pleasure indistinguishable; and then, the orgasm having gone as quickly as it had overtaken, I collapsed across her, murmuring, feeling the bird of that orgasm depart with swoops and weird cries, now echoes in the room.

She kissed me on the cheek. "You see," she said, "you see?" and gave me a breast out of her nightgown. I opened my mouth, put my teeth on it, felt the nipple arc into mouth, and she gave me suck, then in the close spaces of the bed, and I took it deeply until the rising began again. "You see?" she said, "you see?" And I guess I did see. I must have come three or four times that night—no, it may only have been two—but it was constant. I was at her in those spaces for hours and hours and no sense of transition from one state to the next—

"You're crazy," she said, "you're all crazy. You believe your lies. You wouldn't know the difference between truth and lies if it were shown to you, because that's the kind of people you are."

You do not forget things like that.

Merrick and Henry, Merrick or Henry, whichever or both of you are on duty today (I have not looked up from this for several hours; I am filmed with sweat; it is pouring into my rheumy old eyes), you simply do not forget things like that under any circumstances.

Today the weekly visit from Doctor Goodenough. I do not know if it is weekly, my chronological sense having slipped along with so much else recently, but it *feels* weekly; the intervals of light and dark are consistent enough, and the rhythms of Doctor Goodenough working out their dark loose counterpoint to those of Merrick and Henry, and the unseen stalkers of the night appear to be consistent unto that cycle. I think that it is a week. Under Henry's observation, Goodenough gave me the standard fitness and reflex test, tapping me here and there, examining pupils with his concentrated light for incipient or progressive brain damage; slammed me in the stomach; felt thinly of a biceps; and then, with a gesture, ordered Henry out of the room—the bedroom, I should add, in which these examinations are always conducted. Henry was not pleased with this, remaining in position, his lips locked to sullenness.

"Please," Doctor Goodenough said, "I want to talk to the president alone."

"He's not supposed to be left alone at any time," Henry said, "the orders—"

"I make the orders. I make the orders here and I am telling you to leave."

Henry looked up at the ceiling, then in an odd gesture directly at me, as if looking for corroboration and support. "Isn't it true that I'm supposed to stay?" he said weakly, almost piteously—piteousness not being an element of the personality which I have ever associated with Henry—"isn't that clear?"

"You have been told to leave, Henry—"

"I take my orders from him—"

"No," Doctor Goodenough said, "you do not take your orders from him, you take your orders from me," and with an exasperated gesture, slammed his little black bag closed, the report quite galvanizing in the little spaces of the room and quite discomfited by sitting like a suitcase opened for inspection on the bed, mute baggage.

I said, "All right, Henry, I am asking you to leave now. I'm ordering you to do so." Henry, standing, shaking his head. "I'm sure that the doctor is right," I said, surprised at my calmless and reflexive lucidity; really, it had been so long since I have given orders of any sort—little spiteful, senile outbursts not counting—that it was strange to see that I still had the power of command. The old, reasonable tone was in my voice, the steel and calm, the suspicion of threat, I sounded quite as well as I ever had before. A good

39

day for me, and Henry, shaking his head, quit the bedroom instantly, mumbling to himself, snapping the door closed, leaving Goodenough and myself confronting one another in a posture on the bed that instantly converted itself to restlessness. Lying naked, I pulled the covers over me for some protection while Goodenough's gaze flicked politely away; then he said, "I might as well get right to the point. You know that your condition is not improving."

"Yes," I said. I have already said that this was a lucid day for me. I felt quite in focus and as a matter of fact able to discuss my condition, as if Wild Bill Springer were some unfortunate in the next room. I am aware of that.

"You still have your good periods, but they're coming further and further apart now, and it's almost impossible to regulate for them. You're out of control; it's not necessary to tell you that, is it? We can't really find a balance; it's hit or miss now. More and more we've just got to increase the dosages, but that's no good either, your tolerance levels are just moving way up. I don't think that we can promise any sort of control at all, and the periods between lucidity are going to be greater and greater."

Goodenough is in his fifties, I imagine; he comports himself with a strange youthfulness. And underneath the sagging outlines of his face, the corruption of the flesh, one can see a wasted, eager youth, which he indeed must have been in 1960 or thereabouts, but this illusion has never comforted me. He is what he is and what he symbolizes is dreadful. Nevertheless, feeling that I understand him as I do, there is a kind of control. I know nothing whatsoever of his personal life. I know nothing of his professional background either; to be quite honest, he was merely assigned to me. Nevertheless I have no reason to believe that he is anything other than competent, although he has a clumsy hand with an injection, a real shudder on the needle, which more than once or twice has brought foaming blood to the surface when he has slipped the controlling drugs into the pathways.

"We might have to face the question of institutionalization again," he said to me quite seriously.

"I have faced it."

"I'm willing to discuss this with you. As a matter of fact, Mr. President, I have demanded from the first the right to discuss all of this with you objectively. I have too much respect—"

"Institutionalization is out," I said. "We have already decided that. They have already decided that."

"It could be done very quietly," Goodenough said. "We originally, all of us, feared that it might become public knowledge, but things have changed a good deal in the last six months. There's much less interest and attention than there has been in the past. In fact, you're practically forgotten. In fact," he said excitedly, "in fact, it could be said that it would be possible to arrange it with a minimum of publicity and in an institutional framework—"

"I don't want to be institutionalized," I said. It was like telling a child that despite the logic of his arguments, he *still* could not fly. Goodenough settled back in position, the flickering little activity within subsiding. It occurred to me that he was not a bad person and that in many ways he was a creditable individual, and therefore it was not his fault, not strictly speaking his fault at all that I

41

hated him. He did not want to be this way any more than I wanted to be in my own position, but on the other hand questions of role dominate. They always must dominate.

"It's just a matter of going day by day then," Goodenough said. "I'm being quite frank with you here. What I'm doing is not professional at all." A disturbed look flicked once again across his face. "I could get in very serious trouble for talking this way with you. I'm just supposed to administer and that's that."

"I do understand. I do appreciate that."

"But I feel that you're capable of understanding your own situation and of reaching a decision. Of making decisions on it."

"How long do I have?" I said.

"Before what?"

"Before I won't be able to function at all. Before the periods of lucidity are gone. Before I'm not capable of thinking."

He shook his head. "There's no way of determining that," he said, "no one can make judgments like that. We can try, keep on trying to hit a balance. It's possible that we may find some combination—"

"But you haven't yet."

"No."

And you think that there's going to be a steady decline. That you won't be able to hit this balance because you haven't already."

"Yes," he said, "yes, that's pretty much the way I see it. Of course, it's possible that you may find the balance on your *own*. The metabolism is a very subtle and tricky thing. We're trying all kinds of combinations and possibilities, and at some level the body itself may find an accord."

"But you doubt it."

"Yes," he said, "I doubt it very much." He leaned over and picked up his bag, dangled it from his wrist in that curiously effeminate fashion. "It wouldn't be that bad," he said, "I mean, you could find a situation in an institutional framework where you'd be able to do as much as you're doing here, maybe even more. There wouldn't be any more restriction of your activities, and you'd have advantages—"

"No," I said. "I will not do that. That is one thing which is absolutely clear. The president of the United States is not going to be institutionalized."

"I didn't say you had to be," Goodenough said with a rather sullen expression. "I've tried to avoid it from the first. That's the reason I'm here. But there is much less public attention now than you might think, and it would be possible—"

"That is all," I said. My fingers began to coil and uncoil. An image hit me broadside; I could leap from my posture, spring on Goodenough and attempt to strangle him, dig my long and graceless fingers into his throatline and start to throttle him, watch the blood drain out of his head, his face becoming a bulbous white in the light of the room, his floppings and thrashings as he fell before me like a fish on the carpet, dribbling out his life on the rug . . . but no, no. It would not work. If I had had the strength to have done this, I would not have been in this position to begin with, but instead would have been in an entirely different position sitting *ex-partum* in the Senate, giving wise and mellow, only slightly ironic, dictums on the state of the nation, offering my wise and distant counsel to those who would gather around me, perhaps acting as the moderator of my own internationally acclaimed television presentation.

Yes, any number of things could have happened, but none of them did, because a funny thing happened on the way toward senescence, and just like that I found myself beginning to lurch out of control. It was Peoria all over again, except that Peoria had been merely a symbol, a metaphor for everything that was to follow—sliding, sliding out of contact, my eyes drooling their way down Goodenough's lapels and down to his pants legs, my mouth falling open to slackness.

What a disgusting old fool you are, disgusting. The elements of my revulsion were so interesting that I felt myself dwindling into a little place in which one by one I picked out all the pieces of my persona that repelled me the most, all of the reasons why I was despicable, evil, weak, repulsive . . . and in that eave of self, after some passage of time, I tumbled and tumbled, coming out of it to find that Goodenough was gone and that faithful Merrick had returned to the room.

"Do you want to do some more work today, Mr. President?" he said—I thought that he was laughing at me—"or would you prefer to rest?" Surely he was laughing at me; he knew of my condition; he and Goodenough had consultations all the time, explicit instructions delivered.

"No," I said, "no, I do not want to do any more work today; no there is no more work today; no there is nothing more at all today." In a way I blame Goodenough for everything and in a way for nothing at all. "No more work today, Merrick, I must stay in the bed and close my eyes and disgust myself."

Now the question of the curse was clear, no one could avoid it anymore. Now the question was, was it a hundred-year curse, terminating out on the point of 1960? Or was it merely to go on and on, presidents elected in years ending with *0* dying and dying in office? First Lincoln, then Arthur, then McKinley and Wilson, Roosevelt stroking out in a garden, and Kennedy of course, which had added a whole new element to the situation, more McKinley than McKinley himself. But what the mystics (who were very active that year) wanted to decide was whether it was merely a hundred-year cycle or whether more likely it would go on and on, this curse on the presidency, and every twenty years on the dot the proud inauguree would have to juggle thoughts of pride and power with blacker images of fire or water, pestilence or disease while working his way through the ritual ironies of his address. Hope raised the issue herself years before, but of course I was not thinking of it at that time, my own modest ambitions secreted below the level of purpose, being largely invisible even to myself in those benign years, and the incumbent being apparently well settled into his eight-year course. But when the incumbent announced that he would not run for a second term late in '79 and did it in a fashion which seemed to block off any forced renomination, little tender shoots and flowers of purpose began to gather in my mind for the first time, and in the strangely lacklustre field of candidates that emerged at that time, I seemed to have as good a chance as any.

"You know why nobody really wants it," Hope said. "They're thinking of the curse."

"The curse?" I said. I had not even thought of it until that time. "What curse?"

"The twenty-year curse," she said and went on to explain. And of course once she did, it all came reeling back—or should I say exploding—into consciousness.

"Well," I said, "that certainly has nothing to do with me."

"It has everything to do with you; it means that if you really want it, you can get it," she said. "You don't think that anyone really wants this now, do you? When you come right down to it, you'll have a clear field. Anyone who announces early and campaigns hard for this can have it. Everyone will get out of your way. No one really wants it, but you should be aware of it." Hope had none of Eunice's problems. Second wives in politics rarely do; they know exactly what they are getting and are, in fact, titillated by it. This is one of my generalizations.

"It's just a silly coincidence," I said, "it's just happenstance." I was then in what I like to recollect as my rational period: rational possibilities, rational solutions, a Johnsonian precision in the cultivated majority leader who did not believe in myths, dreads, phantoms, spirits, or the onslaught of the uncontrollable, except as it might have affected him in his fantasy life or in certain vagrant impulses of sexuality. I don't think that anyone takes this seriously at all.

"No?" she said. "You don't think so? Have you

ever heard of a president retiring in mid-term, announcing that he wouldn't run again?"

"Coolidge," I said, "Coolidge announced that."

"What does Coolidge have to do with it?" she said, "Coolidge was no president, he was a man who inherited. He ran again because he didn't even know what he was getting into, but once he did—when he did—he found that he didn't like it. He never campaigned for the nomination; it never interested him. We're talking about a man who dedicated his life to the presidency, who won, who gave it four years—"

"It's ridiculous," I said again. "I don't even think that he knows about it. I can't imagine—"

She gave me that look. Hope always had a way of giving me a look—in certain aspects of light, in certain ways, a look which undercut me completely, which turned a situation around and wheeled me back upon myself. At one time I thought that this was an affectionate gesture, that it came out of affection and understanding and a kind of deep subterranean closeness which is exhibited in only the very best of marriages; but later on I learned that this was not so and that the look was always the same, what it had been for twenty-nine years, annihilative. But of course as age burned her flesh and attractiveness away, duplicity was harder to come by and her purposes franker. She said, "A man like this? *This* president? Do you really think he doesn't know exactly what he's doing and why he's doing it? It could only be that. He's aware of it."

"That's ridiculous," I said again, "that's absolutely ridiculous. Why, a president of the United States! A man doesn't abandon national office because of a superstition, because of a bunch of mystical nonsense." But later on, as the season progressed, I began to make the slow, cautious changes in cloakroom and party. (There are ways to put a nomination together which are too subtle even for the refined mechanism of these tapes.)

You don't think that I'm really going to give you information like this, do you Henry? Why, you could use it and run for president yourself someday—not that this would necessarily be a bad thing, I mean, there *have* been presidents worse than you would make, Henry. At least your reach would not exceed your grasp; and you know that in your heart you are a very stupid man, although a very competent male nurse. To be sure. To be sure, Henry, you are a competent male nurse.

Putting together the filaments of possibility slowly—Georgetown here, consultation at the statehouse there, discreet meeting with contributors over in that corner, conferences on the floor of the Senate, working the press and milking the media for the little bit which was due me—I could see that what Hope had said was right, that what she had constructed was not indeed of whole cloth but had some basis, because I could see that the curse—I began to think of it in a very feminine way, masculine curse of the presidency, feminine curse of the month—the curse was very much on everyone's mind. And instead of what we could have expected—eager scurrying and jockeying of candidates—there was a vast sighing reluctance from anyone to emerge from the corners, even those who would have been felt most likely.

As you note, Henry, I am keeping the use of proper names to a minimum here—I do not think that the transcribed tapes of an ex-Chief of State should be a place to exchange old gossip or pay off old personal debts and animosities. But rather I like to think that it is the twenty-first century nearly upon us for which I am dictating, and these memoirs will have far more value if personalities are suppressed and vague descriptions are inserted for names . . . of course, I am perfectly aware, Henry, there being no nonfool like a senile nonfool, that I may be accused, as other presidents have been in their authorized memoirs, of concealing personalities and descriptions for their own sake—out of cowardice, that is to say—and the desire to paint a nice image even if retrospectively. Not so, Henry. Not so at all. Between this excellent microphone and my own lips, there is a complete collaboration, one of utter understanding; I can say anything to it, it (it knows me) will absorb. There is nothing holding me back from the dissemination of names, events, dates, places but my own sense of decorum—that and advancing arteriosclerosis, of course. My recall is not what it should be.

But what's-his-name did not seem to want the nomination; and the young fool from Kansas stuck to fund-raising only in his own state, for his own reelection campaign; and the boob from New York, who is to this date in the Senate, did not as expected come out but rather stayed to his own bovine mutterings; and the closet case from the Midwest, Governor of one of our more populous states, did not himself show the proper inclination to make that gesture—fusing courage, the moment, and the man in that great lunge toward the turn of the century (I am quoting him here; I am not incapable of creating such rhetoric). And as we scurried down toward July, the field of us, it became increasingly apparent that the field was *me*, that of all of us, that is to say, the only one whose efforts were at all serious and whose conviction seemed to match his possibility was the distinguished majority leader of the U.S. Senate himself. Not even the president wanted it.

I think at heart all of us thought that he did. All of us convinced ourselves, I think, that he was merely waiting for the Right Psychological Moment to reverse himself, to declare that he could no longer withstand the cries of a grateful and devoted citizenry and that he would, after all, accept the renomination. It might have been the specter of that, a sitting president and our reluctance to offend him, to seem too much like sniffers of carrion which held down efforts at the nomination; on the other hand, his sincerity, as we staggered into the homestretch, even seemed to increase. He had pulled out of all the primaries; and somewhat reluctantly I made the rounds from New Hampshire to South Dakota to Oregon, finding to my own astonishment that opposition was lackadaisical; and by two months before convention time, with only a minimum of attention to the campaign, meanwhile spending my time in the Senate building a Working Image, I was the leading candidate for the nomination by default. It is best to pick one's spots in the primaries cautiously, Henry, it is not possible to win them all, no mortal man can do that, but by carefully preselecting and concentrating efforts, it is possible to win all those that one enters, and this gives an impression of invulnerability. I hope you are paying close attention to this course in practical politics.

Finally, not three weeks before the convention was to convene—it was in Las Vegas that year, if you recall—I was summoned to the White House, not with the rest of the leadership but *in flagrante, in solitaro* (to reach for the little bit of Latin; not too hard, it comes back), and there I met the president alone for the first time in several years—or since a notable, rather drunken incident which I will not discuss and which had occurred in 1970 in circumstances different for each of us. It was the first time I had seen him alone since then, ten years almost to the date, and I was surprised to find how little the office had touched him. Always in the Congressional conferences or at state occasions, it had been at a distant remove under conditions favorable to him, but here in the Oval Office, seeing him face to face and without benefit of lighting or assistants, he still looked surprisingly youthful, although of course there was a rather sullen cast to his face and his jowls sagged. Still, what is there to say? None of us get any younger ever, and he was a man close to fifty years; but next to my rather careworn seventy, he looked as youthful as ever, if not more so.

I sat before him rather restlessly, my hands folded in a strange and unaccustomed primness and tried to keep the anticipation out of my gestures as I leaned toward him.

"I suppose you wonder why I asked you to come here alone, Bill," he said to me.

"Well no," I said, "not exactly. I imagine that you wanted to tell me first that you have decided to take renomination after all, and as a courtesy to me, you're telling me this directly."

He shook his head. "No, that isn't so. My withdrawal, Bill, was absolute, and I'm not reconsidering under any circumstances. If you want the nomination, you can have it. You're certainly in

51

front; you've done a good job here, and I wouldn't do anything to stop you. I don't think that anyone would."

"You're not going to run," I said. "It's true, it's really true; you're going to retire."

"Not retire," he said with that famous and well-beloved smile, which at close range was all props and greasepaint, like actors observed in dress rehearsal under poor lighting from the first row orchestra. "No, I think I'll write my memoirs or something. I've asked you to come, Bill, to find out if you really want this job. You can have it if you want it, you know. The nomination is pretty much in the bag, and I've done a fairly good job of holding the party together. If I make the nomination speech for you—I probably will—and if you play your cards right and I do a little campaigning mostly by staying here and out of your way, I think you should win this by about sixty-forty or at least fifty-five forty-five. The point is, do you want it?"

I had never thought about it. This is true; until that moment it had never occurred to me to think whether or not I had wanted it. I had never thought about the majority leadership, about the House, about the state senate. I had thought about nothing. All of politics is tropism; you go where you can, that is the key. One moves toward vacancy. Metaphysics has never been my strong point. It was a strangely disquieting question. I should say that metaphysics had up until *then* not been my strong point—now, along with urinary behavior, it is clearly one of my obsessions.

"I don't know," I said looking at him, "it's an opportunity, isn't it? I mean, I guess I want it."

"You've never thought about it."

"Not seriously. I never thought that I'd be president, so why worry about it? It never occured to me that you wouldn't want to run again, and by that time, I'd be seventy-four years old. Even now, I'm seventy. What's a seventy-year-old man doing, running for the presidency? It's ridiculous," I said quite frankly. "But no one else was there, so I did it."

"Don't worry about seventy. Geriatric science is wonderful. They can keep you going, Bill, until you're eighty or ninety. You'll have less trouble being president than you would have being retired. But do you really want it?"

"I don't know," I said, "I guess so. I guess if you gave me time to think about it, I'd decide that I wanted it—yes. I mean, it's just about as far as you can go, isn't it?"

"You'd be surprised."

"It's nothing that I couldn't handle."

"There are problems, Bill," the president said vaguely.

"I'm aware of the problems. I know what's happening. But the Algerian situation is pretty quiet now, I think we've made good strides on Syria, and the monetary situation is working out. Domestically it's no good, but when has it ever been good? We're always going to be dealing with vigilantism—but even there we're making strides."

"This isn't a civics lecture, Bill," the president said, and stood, stretched, looked out his window toward the monument. "I'm sure that you're quite capable, and of course most of our problems are insolvable, they just take on different names as we go along." He paused and looked at me. "Have you thought of the curse?" he said.

I shifted in my seat, looked up at him mildly. "Curse?"

"Don't be a fool. It's just the two of us here and I'm not taping. There haven't been any tapes here for five years, Bill. Nothing will be held against you. You have thought about it, haven't you?"

"I've thought about it," I said.

"Well? What do you think of it?"

"I don't think anything," I said. "It's a historical accident. If it isn't a historical accident, *I* can't change it. Who can? How can any of us? What can we do, not have a president? Not have an election?"

"People were thinking of that," he said lightly, cracking his knuckles above his head. "That was one of the alternatives which was raised. Seriously," he continued, looking at me, "in '77 we saw all of this coming along. We had conferences about it. We decided that nothing could be done, that almost anything would look like a meddling with the process or a coup d'etat; and after what we had been through with Nixon, we couldn't afford stuff like that anymore. But it was discussed, of course. Putting the election off a year or even calling for a referendum on the question. Getting a caretaker in or resigning and appointing the vice-president."

"That's ridiculous," I said.

"It was my idea, Bill," he said, "I was the one who saw this coming. Do you think it's a coincidence that we can't really get a candidate, that a seventy-year-old senator looks like he's getting it by default? It's even worse with the opposition. They've got a couple of governors, and both of them are trying to back out in favor of the other one. It's really an embarrassing situation, both of

54

them trying to jump. I have good intelligence. Of course, I always knew this office was good for something."

"Are you afraid of the curse?" I said. "Is that the reason you're withdrawing?"

"What do you think?" he said, and then sat down abruptly and leaned over the desk. "If I really was, do you think I'd tell you? Of course not," he said after a pause, "that's all mysticism, superstition, and nonsense. How could a president of the United States be influenced by garbage like that? It would make a terrible impression on the populace. I don't even read the INTELLIGENCER."

"So you are," I said, rather wonderingly I might add. There must have been rather a youthful disillusionment in my aged voice. "You're really influenced—"

"I didn't say that," he said, much more sharply, sitting abruptly, moving in his seat to command an imposing view of the monument, giving me a view equally imposing of his shoulder blades. He wheeled back to me then. "I didn't say that at all and that isn't what I called you here for. If you are going to be president—and at this point you seem to be as likely a candidate as we have—then you might as well be apprised of certain situations you'll be facing that you might not be aware of. That was the reason for this."

"I'm the majority leader," I said. "Don't you think that your own majority leader—"

"I'm my own majority leader," he said, "nobody is responsible for that but myself. Do you think you're told everything, Bill?"

"No," I said, feeling constraint now, the whole situation reeling around, I did not like the situation; I liked none of it—the sullenness of his man-

55

ner, the puffiness of his face, the strange, glazed expression of his eyes, a certain arrogance in his manner, the threat in his bearing, the hint that matters had been held back from me—and it was as if I could see pouring out of him some aura, some veritable, palpable haze of fear. It must have been the aura of fear itself in the room to which I was reacting, which was contributing to the hostility of his manner.

"There are things about the nuclear situation that we've pretty well managed to keep hidden Bill," he said. "I don't think the press has gotten hold of any of this, at least the national press; there might be a few here and there in Washington who have sources and have gotten a leak, but not the nationals. It would be a disaster if they got it, but I don't think they will. There are problems with the nuclears, Bill. We've lost control of a couple of the plants."

"What?" I said. "I don't know what you're talking about." Nobody thought about nuclears anymore. The strategic arms limitation along with what China and Russia had been doing to one another in the late '70's had pretty well taken any consciousness of nuclears away from us. We just didn't think about them in those gentle days, Henry. If one generation had grown up thinking about nuclear holocaust, then another one was utterly unconscious even of its definition. And I admit that when he started talking about *nuclears*, it was necessary for me to send my mind momentarily skittering back ten to fifteen years in plane of reference, simply so that I knew what he was talking about. I didn't know what he was talking about.

"I've got to tell you something very serious now

Bill," the president said. "It's a situation with which I've been living for some time. It's something you're going to be living with too, and if you really want to campaign for the presidency, if you want this office, you're entitled to know exactly what you're heading into. You won't like it Bill—I don't think that anyone would like it. But you've got to know."

"I still don't know what this is," I said, but some chill—or maybe the word is apprehension—had brushed me as with a bird's wing for the first time; then I felt that I was moving close or closer into understanding. "Why don't you tell me?"

"We've lost control of two of the piles, Bill," the president said. "They've been taken over; the entire installation has been taken over in both cases. And they've fallen out of our control for the moment. It's a stalemate because they don't want any publicity and we can't go in and get them. But they're just waiting, I think; they're just waiting for the proper time, and then they're going to hold us up."

"Hold us up? Hold us up for what?"

"You still don't understand, Bill," the president said. "I never would have thought that—I mean we've had our disagreements and so on—but I never would have thought that you would simply miss the point like this. They've got hold of two nuclear installations, atomic power plants—don't you understand? And they—"

"Who are *they?*"

He waved me off. "Don't worry about who they are right now," he said. "If I gave you one name or I gave you another, would it make any difference? They give themselves a name, do you think that the name means anything? We know who they are too, but that's just biography; it doesn't solve anything; it doesn't make us any more likely to deal with the situation considering what they've got. They're just biding their time and then—"

"Blackmail?" I said, making the leap. "Is that it? They're going to hold us up—"

"The whole planet," the president said, nodding at me encouragingly, his eyes very bright and deep in his face, "the whole fucking planet. Do you see what I mean, Bill? It isn't the curse. I mean, *this* is the curse."

We sat there for a while.

I didn't know sex (I mean, I did know sex, of course, I did in the clinical, oracademic sense of the word), but I really didn't know it or had forgotten what it was (take your pick) until Hope came along. It had been so long—oh, my God—it had been so very long, and I had not even thought of it, what with the responsibilities and distractions of my office.

"Don't be a pig," Eunice had said, "you're forty-two years old. Isn't it time you grew up? That kind of thing isn't for us anymore, we had all of that; we had our time, and now our time is past; and I won't tolerate it. Separate bedrooms, please."

I was naive, of course. I should have understood what it meant, that this was not normal, that it is impossible for a marriage to shut off sex unless something is deeply, tragically wrong with the marriage at the heart and that something has

58

been lost forever. As a matter of fact I *did* know it, but what was the difference? I didn't find her that attractive anymore myself; she was ugly, as a matter of fact, all the ugliness to the surface.

And then there were the random adulteries. Don't look so shocked, Merrick; I didn't say that I had no sexual outlet—of course I did, everybody in Washington does somewhere, somehow. There are secretaries, speechwriters, PR gals, teachers at colleges, newspaperwomen, conventions ... it is impossible for a U.S. Senator not to have a satisfactory sex life unless he is a eunuch, in which case he can certainly find himself a pimp or set of them catering exclusively to the needs and desires of eunuchs, whatever they may be. I was a U.S. Senator, Merrick; I was a powerful U.S. Senator —the majority leader—and reasonably attractive, considering all of the cosmetic benefits which can be heaped upon one who has access to the corridors of power. I am not speaking of the routine adulteries—now they meant nothing. I thought they were entirely satisfactory, and in their own way, they were. They certainly kept me away from Eunice's door—a consummation devoutly to be wished by the two of us—and greatly lowered the level of tension in our dying marriage.

It is true—nothing will keep a dying marriage going any longer or any better than casual adultery. I would feel much better about Eunice in the aftermath of my fucking, in and out, three pumps and come, fall drooling to one feminine shoulder or the next and the arc of breast under my stomach; the dead motions of my flaccid tool against her in the act of withdrawal would convince me that Eunice was right—there was something ridiculous to sex; at the very best it was trivial, a custom really, a series of twitches and tropisms not unlike the tropism of politicians toward higher and higher office. If this was all she was denying me, then she was denying me very little. Of course, I am talking about the aftermath—of aftermaths there were many. But for every aftermath, there is of course an anticipation, a conjugation; I would not think this way at the point of entrance, but instead all fire in my fucking would move to fuck and come as quickly as possible . . . not to disgrace Eunice, of course. If I would do it quickly, I would not disgrace her.

I want you to know that I am talking about the constancy of my life here for years and years, no compression (although through the miracle of tape and incontinent babblings, it is possible to compress a great deal into a very little), but rather a condition which went on and on—it must have been this way for seven years, seven or eight of not too careful, not too joyous but always sufficient fucking. And it might have gone on and on—in fact it *did* go on and on, until Hope changed all of that by showing me something that I had clearly forgotten, perhaps because I had chosen not to recollect it, perhaps because it had seemed worth the forgetting: she showed me the power of the flesh. The entwinement of connection or perhaps it is confection I am thinking of connection/confection oh the words are very hard sometimes to disassociate enjambment in the mind being as it is in the progressively senile but then again the sounds are pretty, the sense is in the sounds as was once pointed out about political rhetoric and oh my God the collions we had, the small and terrible explosions of the flesh, flowering, flowering.

60

I must concede the point; I must approach the truth; I think in certain angles that my second wife was a piece of ass the cunt. Even I could think of it; she was able to do certain things in her own bedroom, contrive certain angles of light, resistance, costumes, makeup (which as the light-show developed would make her seem beautiful). And it was many, many years and only at a different stage of my life when I realized that she was not beautiful, that everyone was right and I was wrong; that it was not her special beauty I was seeing but merely the same raddled face and complexion that she had worn before her thirtieth birthday, and which everyone else knew. Nevertheless, I was entranced. We are not talking about an adolescent now, we are talking about a forty-three-year-old man in the flower of his manhood—and my, oh my, how I flowered!

How I flowered underneath and above her making all of the changes in her room. (It was always her room in the hotel; it was the best and most discreet place, she said; she wouldn't risk anything by going elsewhere, and only in Washington could I absolutely control my schedule and my companions; she was very thoughtful and protective even from the first—I thought it was altruism; it was only later on that I realized how entirely clever she had been.)

Going into her was entering knowledge itself, her yielding, springing past the initial softness into a resistance harder than any I had ever known; push harder and open her up a bit more, meet more stone, push harder and inch so a little further. I never knew a woman it was harder to fuck or whom the entering took longer. But finally, inch by inch, I would get into her small, gutted cluster of a hole, her breasts crowding all around me, huge hard flowers reeking of the hothouse ... and pounding in and out of her, I would then feel that accomplishing penetration was of a more profound nature than anything which I might accomplish on the floor, never was anything so worthwhile in my life or so worthy of pride (if there had only been someone to brag to) than actually getting inside this woman.

"Oh, my," she had said in the confessional of sex time and again, "oh, my, that's wonderful. There's never been anyone who was ever able to get all the way inside me. I've been to doctors and all that and they say that there's nothing wrong, but I've always been afraid that there *was* something wrong. Isn't it wonderful? Isn't it a wonderful thing to know after all of this time that there *isn't!* But it would take a man, it would take a real, real man, to be able to do that Bill; oh, you're wonderful," putting an enormous breast in my mouth while I sucked and banged away, still imprisoned within her (she was as difficult to leave as she was to enter, but who in God's name would want to leave something like that?) and working myself toward another peak—and if you don't think this was heady stuff, you are quite seriously wrong.

You are wrong indeed to misjudge off the page on which you will read this—assuming transcription will be accomplished. But somehow I wonder if they will actually permit a typist to get hold of these tapes and do the job; but one thing is sure— I am not going to. I can barely hold my fingers out straight, let alone consider transcription. If you don't think that was something I needed badly at the time, exactly what I needed, as a matter of fact; and although out of the boudoir the language of sex may seem silly and rather naive, you would be equally naive not to understand context and situation. What works here would not work there; what works within the boudoir—while not quite passing for a Nobel Peace Prize acceptance speech —can do things in those confines that the laureate's mumblings could never do.

Not to be mistaken about this, I tumbled within her again and again, past excitement, past all rationalization, merely sensation and that rising pressure, that engorgement sliding past level and level of her, the walls of her breaking and opening within me . . . and all of the time, every night of it, returning to my own quarters at some disastrous hour of the morning because the majority leader could not risk any scandal in his personal life. It is one thing to make inching and drastic entrance into a passionate woman at midnight; it is quite another to come staggering home at three in the morning, a certain burning shame overwhelming retrospection. . . . Merrick or Henry, it must be understood, there are certain contradictions possible in one's personal life which cannot be annealed, which cannot be covered over in any way, which simply exist and must be lived with; and this irony, this tension, this gap between the expected and the actual behavior can be said to function as that emptiness from which all true acts of statesmanship may begin.

I may exaggerate. Hyperbole is not unknown to the political act, and there is a certain tendency to overstate. One can attract more attention through overstatement, of course, but it must be said that the politician's overstatement may come only from his need to set larger and larger shocks to the psyche, which enable him to move past reflex to feeling ... only lying will give him feeling, and the lies must become more and more preposterous as time goes on. Furthermore, since he is fundamentally an honest man (it is in search of his honesty that he has sought politics), the politician, or at least the majority leader, tends to believe his own lies—so there is no longer a question of duplicity here but rather one of psychopathology.

Politicians are not liars. I was not a liar. I have never been a liar. I took myself to be passionately linked with Hope Johnson; I was truly and deeply in love with her ... if this were not so, why would I skulk to her apartment night after night, risking more and more, increasingly careless of my responsibilities or notoriety, simply to plumb those depths once again, to feel the oozing release of her cunt as I wedged myself in there, gasping? She was never any easier to penetrate. She remained tight from beginning to end. I thought at the outset that it was titillating; it was only much later that I came to understand that the woman was absolutely impenetrable. I was not dealing with her cunt but with her personality.

Honesty commended me to make a full statement of the situation to Eunice. Nothing else could be done in the circumstances. I felt that she was entitled to know what I wanted. It never occurred to me for an instant not to divorce her and to marry Hope Johnson immediately. I would have had it no other way. Politicians, from an excess of promoting convention, are the most conventional of people. My life itself is testament to this.

"It is all finished, Eunice," I said to her in that recollected conversation. "Eunice, it is all over. I must be permitted to leave. It will be better for both of us if you permit me."

"I won't," she said, "you are filth. You are lies. You are deceit and moral waste," and so on and so forth. I will not repeat already transcribed material; I have a good recollection of what I have and have not put down on these tapes, my recollection being much better than I am given credit for possessing.

"I will make it hell for you," she said, "I will tie you up in the courts and take it to the newspapers and make statements as to exactly what kind of person you are—and by the time that I am done with you, you would not be electable even for the Illinois lower house again. That's what I'll do to you."

"Be reasonable, Eunice," I said, "be reasonable. I'm going to do it no matter what you say."

"You'd give up your political career? You wouldn't know what to do without it—"

"I will give up my political career," I said. "I will give up everything. I am trying to be honest, Eunice. This is more important to me than anything else."

"You are a liar."

"I am not a liar. I am going to do it in any case. I am going to do exactly what I want and be damned; and if you understand that, you can make it easier for both of us, Eunice." I had not called her *Eunice* in many years. I had not used her name for more time than I could remember. Perhaps that was part of the difficulty; I had lost any sense of her as a person. She was merely a device, an obstacle. One cannot say. That was part of it, but there might have been another part as well.

"You think you're the Duke of fucking Windsor," she said, "marrying the woman you love. That's what you're going to try; you'll make a radio speech—"

"No," I said, "no more. I cannot take this anymore." I stood. "I am going to leave, Eunice. I am not going to come back. I will take out what I can take out now and the rest I will send for."

"You can do whatever you want. If you disgrace me, I'll ruin you forever, that's all. Do you understand that?"

"I'm leaving," I said again. There was nothing else to say. One reaches a point stock-still in the center in which there is nothing, absolutely nothing to be done; even the devices of further movement seem fruitless.

It was with an effort that I turned away from her. "I'm very sorry," I said. "I didn't want it to be this way. I didn't intend it to happen, but it just did, Eunice. People don't remain the same. Everything changes around them and they aren't what they were when they started. It has nothing to do with you."

"Yes it does," she said shockingly. "Look at me," and I looked at her, saw the bleaking, aging, ruined stones of her face. "You blame me for Arthur," she said, "that's always been it."

I gasped. I could not believe it—the audacity. There are certain things so improbable that it is impossible to find any attitude of confrontation leading perhaps to some explication of the popular effects of the assassination. I am only guessing. I claim no expertise in this area. "That's ridiculous," I said finally. "Eunice, that's ridiculous."

"You've always held it against me. You've felt it was my fault from the first."

I shook my head, staring at her. "Eunice," I

said, "Arthur died of cancer. There was nothing to be done. No one can be blamed for this; it was simply something in the genes—"

"That's what I mean," she said, "in the genes. You blame me. You think that he inherited it from me."

I did not know what to say. You go through the convolutions and movements of life for a long time, decades perhaps, living within that shell of mortality which is (I will swear this) as liberating as constricting, and something comes then which completely punctures and makes you understand that all of the time you have lived under a misapprehension. That the shell was not cover but mere translucence for something unimaginable outside of it.

"That's crazy, Eunice," I finally settled for. "That's absolutely crazy. Arthur died of leukemia. It could have happened to anyone. It happened to our son. It's a rare but not at all unknown disease of late adolescence, hemolytic leukemia, and it happened to him. It has nothing to do with heredity."

"I know that," she said. "The doctors knew it. Arthur knew it too. But you don't. You didn't then and you still don't. You blame me."

"You're crazy, Eunice," I said again, not as gently. "You're crazy if you believe that I think that."

"First Arthur's gone and now you want to get rid of me. Then you won't remember anything. Then you can start again, as if none of this ever happened."

"I'm leaving," I said. "I am leaving. I cannot listen to this anymore, Eunice. You have got this impossibly wrong, but I can't deal with it. I can't make you see any differently." I was already through the door. "It has nothing to do with Arthur," I said.

"Then you deny your son?"

"What? What is that now?"

"You're just going to leave? You're walking out of here and cutting this off from you, and your son means nothing to you at all. It's like you were never here, like he didn't exist? Do you think you can bury him, Bill, only in this way?"

I did not know what to say. There was nothing to say. "I'll kill myself if you leave, Bill," she said, "do you hear that?"

"But why? Why?" I instinctively took her seriously. I believed her; there was no doubt in my mind at that moment that she would. That was how far she had taken me. It did not occur to me to disbelieve her. If positions were reversed, I might have done the same.

"Because you're leaving me nothing but shame. You're making me look like a fool."

"First you said you'll ruin my career and now you say you'll kill yourself. Which will it be, Eunice? Which do you want to do? Couldn't you try at least for a little consistency?"

"Both," she said, "I'll kill myself and that will ruin your career. I can have it both ways. I'm not inconsistent at all. I've never told anything but the truth. I've been consistent in my own fashion from the first. You're the one who lies. You're the one who changes position."

I saw the humor. Let it be known that I saw the humor. "All right, Eunice," I said at the door, "all right then. You'll kill yourself, and that way you'll ruin my career. You're perfectly consistent. You haven't deviated from your position for a moment. Only I have. You'll have to do it, Eunice," I said.

I could not believe that the woman was serious. Someone who you have lived with for twenty years must be as well known to you as yourself— if not, then you have no insight whatsoever, because there is a fusion, the two of you are the same person after a while, the only separation in anger; and I thought that I knew her well enough.

"You can't be stopped from doing something like that," I said. "You know that if you're serious, I could stay here and argue with you all day, and you still would do it. And if you're not, then it's pointless for me to stay here. And if it's just a threat to hold me, it won't work. It can't possibly work because I'm not going to stay. Not for any reason. It's too late."

I went out of there.

I did not think she was serious, and I think now that she did not think she was serious either. But there are levels and mysteries to motives, which are beyond us; we are the response, the motives, the stimulus; and somewhere in that great synapse of the Twitch, something may happen which we cannot understand . . . but my judgment was absolute, she could not do it. She could not possibly do it.

If she had—if she had been capable, that was— it would have meant that I had misjudged everything and that the life I had lived was fraudulent. I did not think that there was so much conviction in her. I did not think that there was that level of sincerity; and if there had been, then everything, always, had been wrong, then she would have been a different woman entirely . . . and I should not have left her.

Open on emptiness and pan the sky; move down to the peanut-shell of the limousine in which the Gadget Man sits, his tentacles like a spider's, hunched in one corner surrounded by the white bugs that protect him. Gadget Man is old and cold, bold and mold, lolled rolling into the cache of the limousine, above the dazzling sun, beneath the concrete, and sealed deep into his conviction. Now they come upon him in little waves and ripples of color, disguised as birds fluttering down from the sky, the wavelets of birds rolling over the limousine in which Gadget Man lolled. But he is too bold and cold for them, sees their purpose and knows their cunning; with a cunning of his own extracted from the tomb of himself, Gadget Man reaches inside, the white bugs to his left and right fleeing as he seizes upon the weapon . . . and then he shoots the birds with his fiery gadget concealed within his armor. The birds break, their colors fall away, and they no longer have the form of birds but instead the form of insects. Seeing this, Gadget Man understands something, he understands that birds and guards are the same thing, and what he took to be the protectors are merely another form of that which he must be protected against.

This insight—not to say, the way it registers upon him—drives Gadget Man quite insane. He has not been in the best and most vigorous of health for years; indeed he has been traveling

70

precipitately along the edge, skirting merrily, his limbs crackling with energy as he holds the line between center and disaster. But now, as the birds /insects come upon him, their wings beating like hearts, he is quite mad—oh, indeed, he is quite sufficiently mad—his weapon drooping within his hand, no firearm—not even a clout—but merely a wet, pendulous affliction coming out of the ridges of the hand.

He hits them once! They scurry away; and rising in the seat of the limousine, he hits them twice! And they have reconnoitered; and as he tries to strike them a third time, they have worked out their vicious, cunning, and destructive plan. So they close in upon him, battering and battering.

Despite his bravery, Gadget Man's great heart begins to give out. He feels weakness overtaking him. Looking through some aperture in the attack, he sees the slick web of sky pressing upon him, wheeling his glance left and right, little patches of city; but these are merely interruptions in the panorama of white bodies which press upon him, the limousine picking up speed now, the winds of acceleration transformed to winds of ascension as, tiny gnome pressed against the cushions dwindling in size, the white bugs and birds pressing around him, he becomes at that moment *one of them* and in some coiling and uncoiling of time joins them wheeling in the air. Of course, he sees the Gadget Man himself, Hail Chief, riding to the city.

Spools fouling in the fucking machine; all sense of grasp and control lost; the reels snarling through the loops; loops exploding like confetti; fucking tape all over; surrounded by tape, some of it imprinted, some of it not, the place where it is imprinted covered with streaks submicroscopic —I think the place where it is blank merely blank small streaks—the only trace of what I have left; all matter reduced then to filaments and streaks; everything come down to little marks. Who was it? Beckett? Krapp? Old man in old room talking about life. Am I Krapp? No, am the president of the United States. Repeat that, sir. The president of the United States of America, one hundred and eleventh State of the Union message to the assembled Congress joint houses, great challenges, great years ahead, the American destiny unfurled before us, low taxations, baby boom, strike, manifest, splinter groups, disjointed youth, hungry elders senior power, rage of the aged, increased benefits, lower taxation, loyal oppositition, harmony and balance, equality and justice for all Americans under the law, egalitarianism, the New Dream, the Old Dream, the Old Frontier, the New Frontier, the New Deal, the Fair Deal, the Square Deal, the Nothing Deal, the fouled deal, the fucked up deal, the fucked up, the fucked, the tape, the spittle coming out all over sons of bitches now . . .

"Let me think about it," I said. "You can't come in here, confront me with something like this, expect me to make a decision. I've got to consider, to—"

"That's the same old shit, dads," the representative said. He lit a cigarette with manifest casualness. I could admire what he was doing (fucking Hope was never like fucking Eunice, but in the end it was the same). "You are going to make that decision now. You are not going to go behind closed doors and figure it out with your advisors and give us the same old temporizing shit; you are going to come up right against it now. That's the point. That's the whole point, dads, president or not," and he flipped a match to the carpet always came fast in the first enjambment. "You are going to live in the world just like the rest of us poor fuckers and take your chances."

"It's impossible," I said, "you can't blackmail a whole country. You can't hold up a nation for ransom—"

"Why not?" he said. He puffed on the cigarette. (I always liked to get blown, but how many women can you find who know how to do it? really get it in there and work on it patiently?) "It's working fine so far."

"This is insane," I said—I think I was saying I was insane. "This is madness."

"We'll take it to the media. They're all outside; we'll put the case to them." I looked at him and realized that he was crazy. Not fanaticism, nothing political, this was clear, clinical insanity, and I could measure the effect it was having upon me: it was making me crazy too. The two of us were crazy. Both of us there in the East Wing were madder, but I was madder than he because I was supposed to run the country and I could not get my mind off fucking. All I could think about

73

was fucking. This is impossible for a seventy-three-year-old man, the act of fucking—that is to say, it is almost impossible—but it is very possible to think about; and that was what was on my mind. "Are you listening to me?" he said.

I looked up at him; my eyes must have been quite bleak and staring, watery, as if floating in soup. "What's that?" I said, "what did you say?"

"You crazy old fuck, you're supposed to be the president of the United States. What kind of horseshit is this? We knew you were old, we knew you were sick, but we didn't expect to find someone here lying in a senile stupor, for Christ's sake! What's wrong with you?"

"I'm thinking," I said. "I'm thinking of your offer. The terms and conditions, that is. Didn't you want me to think it over? Isn't that what you said?"

"We asked you to think, not to dream, you crazy old fuck! Hey, what's wrong with you, dads? You cracked or something like that? I mean, you freaking out?"

I stood shuffling my limbs, like canes handled in the wind by a very old man. "I've made my decision," I said. "I think I've made it now."

He backed off. For the first time, there was something hinting at yield in his position. "Okay," he said, "what is it?"

"In due time," I said. "In due time." I walked deliberately away from the desk, went to the windows, looked out at the monument, behind it the spires of the mountains. Once, Hope and I had driven out to a motel there and fucked in view of the Washington Monument. She said that mine felt bigger. (This is the kind of thing you tend to hold on to as you get older and the juices dry out.)

"Not so fast," I said. "I'm an old man, remember? I'm a senile old fuck. We senile old fucks have to think slower, act slower, perform slower than you younger people, so you will forgive me if I take my time. After all, you've got all the time in the world. It's going to be your world."

I had no belief in an afterlife. Despite the appearances of religiosity incumbent upon the office, I have not believed in God or a religious construct for more than fifty years. This makes this taping somewhat easier; in any event I know that it is *finis*, and I will never have to listen to these spools again under any circumstance, which gives me a nice, tight sense of completion—not even to say an ironic impact of some sort. One must take one's ironies where one can get them at eighty years of age. One must take them where one can get them, as a matter of fact, at seventy-three years of age. Ironies for the aged are not unlike orgasms for the young—this is an aphorism which may as well be noted.

Will you note that, Doctor Goodenough? I am glad to see you, as always; yes, things seem a little better today. Let me finish just this little bit of reel here, and I shall be right with you. I had a little trouble with the reels yesterday, but Henry was very helpful and everything is in order today. As a matter of fact, I feel distinctly better. One must take one's ironies where one can get them.

"What do you want?" I said to him.

"You know what we want. We want world government or—"

I made a dismissive gesture. "No," I said,

"that's the cover, the rhetoric. Let's get to the substance. What do you *really* want out of this?"

He shrugged, but his eyes held me close, fastening into me like threads. "Don't worry about that, you son of a bitch," he said, "just worry about yourself."

"But I do," I said. "I worry about myself, and I have to worry about the country too; after all that's the president's role, isn't it? To worry about the country? And I've got to assess your motives in order to be able to assess my own and approach a proper and judicious balance."

"You say you've reached a decision."

"But have *you?*" I said and looked at him levelly. Oh, you would have been proud of me then, doctor—what a man I was. "Have you reached a decision? Do you know what you really want? I don't think that you do."

"You're not talking to an individual. I'm merely a representative. If I leave, there will be another. There is no individual but merely a group whose purposes we enact. There is no decision to be made. The decision has already been made." He was sweating.

"Nonsense," I said quietly, "you are not a representative; you are a person. It is not a group in this room; it is merely you. You are the only one I see. I see no one else. What is your decision?"

"My decision," he said, "my decision, you crazy old fuck, is to walk right out of here now and tell them that you won't negotiate, so we'll have to go ahead. That's my decision." He moved toward the door.

"Is it?" I said, and he held up. "Go on, walk through the door. Walk out. Tell them that nothing has worked, and you've come out with an ulti-

76

matum to destroy because you wouldn't let me talk. Tell them that. Tell your group that. Will they send in another with the same orders?"

"You can't bluff me," he said, "there's no one to bluff. You're dealing with a revolutionary instrument—"

"There are no instruments. There are only people. We talk of institutions and great movements, but at the bottom it is merely sweat and blowing. Don't you understand that, son? Don't you realize that you've got to accept the fact of your humanity?"

"Don't call me son. Don't—"

"You know that you must," I said. "They won't help you on the outside. They're not an instrument, but you are. You are only an instrument to them. They are using you, and they will use someone else in your place. You are in the grip of forces you cannot deny. You had better begin to think and act for yourself, son. They won't help you. They simply don't care what happens to you."

He stood by the door. "You're daring me to leave," he said, "you're really serious about this."

"I am not. I am not doing anything of the sort. I said I had reached a decision. But it is reciprocal. All decisions are reciprocal, and now you must make yours. You must decide what you want to do. I know what I want; have you decided what you—"

"Bastard," he said, "bastard."

"It's your decision," I said, "you see that now. And it always was. From the first. It will never leave your hands; it's your life and you must deal with it."

"Bastard," he said, "dirty bastard."

"Now," I said, "what do you want? Tell me

what you want and touch yourself for the first time."

All right, doctor.

In the night the witch's kiss of sheets surrounding my chin, cutting into the undersurfaces like a blade and opening my eyes, I think I see his hand for just a moment tucking those sheets into my neck: the night attendant. I have never seen him whole, nor the unknown substitute who fills in for him on his mandatory time out, but the sensation of being wrapped in coils of ice by this unseen but benign hand is comforting, it reminds me as it were of the other part of life, the unknown underside into which I descend for twelve hours, half of my life now lying deep in the darkness tended by those unseen, my heart pounding away at its faithful old rhythms, the blood still roiling in the veins, only the light of consciousness extinguished—but the world, dark and mysterious, holding and protecting me, going on.

So it will be when I am no more; so it will be when I am dead. The unseen hands will tuck the sheets around my neck, the presences will float in and out of the grave chambers of the self, and what I know and touch for twelve hours a day now I will touch forever . . . that does not sound so bad now, does it?

On the way back I said, "That whore I fucked, that whore fucked Nathan Leopold. Do you know that?"

"You're crazy," Jim said and giggled. "Maybe you're not crazy, it's possible."

"I'm telling you," I said, "I'm telling you it's the truth. I asked her and she did."

"She said she did?"

I put my hand to my cheek. "No," I said, "she hit me here when I asked her."

And up in the front, giggles, and he said, "Hitting isn't agreeing, hitting is for getting mad. Maybe she didn't like you asking if she fucked Leopold."

"She did, I tell you," I said, "she did. I don't give a damn either way, it doesn't matter to me, but I know that she did and that it did matter." This was a lie, knowing that I had rested in the same place where the Babe had, knowing that the Babe's prick, the prick of a murderer, had churned in the same tunnels that had mine was exciting, no question about this; we had performed the same motions against the same body, and what did that make us? Did it give me any further understanding of his motives? If Leopold could do the same things that I had done in the same way to the same woman, did that mean we were the same? That was what excited me—knowing that we could have been in some way.

But there was no way to carry forth the message before they would question me more closely and possibly think me crazy, so I kept quiet, the car speeding, rubbing my jaw, little darts of pain spreading from the jaw down the chinline and becoming filaments deep in the flesh. And not another word, not another word all the way to Urbana. I never went to a whore again, and that was the only time. Somehow it wouldn't have been the same.

Big, fat sousaphone jabbing like a prick into the car, missing my head by inches, fat red-faced man behind the sousaphone, staggering, bleating, apologizing as they grabbed him by the arms, voice shrieking, eyes tearing, "I didn't mean it, I'm sorry, I didn't mean to do anything." And they whisked him out of sight. I wanted to give him a smile, a nod, some remission. But before I could do so, he was gone. Impossible to make contact, although I certainly tried. One cannot say that I did not try—that is what is known as having in politics the common touch.

"The taping is going to have to stop," Goodenough said, "or at least you're going to have to cut down."

"I can't do that," I said, "this is my whole life now, getting my memoirs down on tape. What else would you leave me? It's got to be done."

He held my wrist, watched my pulse solemnly. "It's taking too much out of you," he said. "I don't like the gross modal signs and the kind of tension under which you're working. You could have a cerebral blowout at any time. You can see that I'm being frank with you, I'm not holding back. The excitement is disastrous."

"I can't stop," I said. "I just can't do that. It's got to be done. This is my mission."

"You're having trouble with the machine," he said. "I understand that you're having trouble more and more operating it. You're spilling tape out of the cannisters and getting it fouled in the recorders."

"That always happened. I'm not mechanically minded."

"At least we should get you a cassette operation of some sort. You could just put a disc into the machine and begin to talk. Cassettes can hold up to ten hours transcription, which is more than reels, no matter how slow the IPS you've got."

"I will not do it," I said. He dropped my wrist; it clattered against my knee. "Bone to bone and to dust we shall returneth. I will not use a cassette. I want to talk into something that I can see. I want to see it mount up. I want to see that I am having an effect. In some ways, I am very old fashioned."

Goodenough smiled, except that he did not smile. "I don't like the signs," he said. "More and more I'm beginning to think that deciding not to institutionalize you was taking too big a risk. That it would have been better to have gone ahead and done it with whatever risk that entailed. This is not safe for you."

"You forget one thing," I said. "I did not want to be institutionalized."

"And now?"

"No," I said, "I do not want to be. I am perfectly content here. I have Merrick. I have Henry and you. I have my tapes and my memoirs and they're all building very nicely. I'm finding some very keen new insights. There are things that I never understood about my two marriages and my administration until I actually got down and started in on this. I feel in many ways that I'm growing as a person."

He smiled at that. I had expected him to. For Goodenough there would only be irony, but for me it was something much closer to insight. It is possible to change. It is possible to grow. Life can and does begin at eighty, as I recall from the radio show of my youth; and besides that, how can anyone elect a point of termination? The underground did and we see where it got them.

"I am doing fine," I said again. "I have no complaints. Now and then I get bitter and depressed. I have my bad days, but don't we all? More and more I feel that I'm being taken care of. I'm getting along. Everything will be all right."

"You don't understand the risks," Goodenough said.

"Of course I do. You've told me."

"And the deterioration," he said grimly. "I told you. I've never lied to you. You're deteriorating rapidly. Yesterday when I was here, it was necessary to triple-dose just to bring you to this point."

"But I feel pretty good now."

"How long do you think it will last?"

"I don't know," I said. Nothing would break the shell of my optimism; I was resolved that this was indeed going to be one of the good days, in fact the very best. Nothing would fracture my calm. "I'm sure that I'll manage. You can keep on triple-dosing me."

"And then quadruple-dosing and then quintuple. But with every rise, the risk increases. The pressure on the cerebral hemispheres. That's where the risk of stroke comes in."

"You have told me that."

"There's no way that we can strike a balance. At least not when you're at a level of such constant excitement, which these tapes seem to be doing to you. If we could get you into a quieter, more controlled—"

"No," I said, "No, I won't go. That's definite."

"All right," Goodenough said. He leaned over, hitched his pants, sucked in his stomach rather self-consciously. "No one can force you to do anything, that's well understood. That was understood from the first. If you want to continue this way, you may. But I warn you," he said, "we may be forced to measure this situation not in months or even weeks but in days. It's perilous."

"I don't think anything different. I'm eighty years old. It would be ridiculous for even a healthy eighty year old to measure out things in months, wouldn't it?"

"I like your philosophy," Doctor Goodenough said. "I admire it. It shows courage and strength. Unfortunately I don't believe it. It's merely the product of drug therapy, and we're getting a very temporary release, a very temporary balance. Fraudulent, I might say. I would like to have the opportunity to listen to some of those tapes. I understand that there are very interesting things. I'm sure that from a medical standpoint, it would be helpful—"

"No," I said, "nobody listens to the tapes." I patted the key in my pocket. There is a key to the study in my pocket, and as far as I know it is the only one. It is possible that Merrick or Henry have a duplicate and that they have in turn handed the duplicate to the unknown night attendants, who open up the study and in the darkside of my life listen to all of the tapes; but I prefer not to believe that this is so. The confidentiality of my memoirs is the key to my sanity at this time. If I did not believe that they were uniquely mine and that no one but myself had access to them as I chose, then it would be impossible to maintain any illusion of self-worth, my ten jou's hold on reality would probably collapse, and I would be no good for anyone at all, least of all myself. "I will not let you listen to the tapes, doctor," I said.

"All right."

"When they are finished and transcribed and published, everyone will have access to them. But right now they must be mine and mine alone."

"That is your decision," Goodenough said. He suddenly seemed seized with awkwardness, his hands fluttering on his knees. "Do you want anything else?"

"Anything what?"

"Anything at all?"

"I have everything I need," I said. "I can't imagine that you could give me anything at all; I mean what I need, you can't give, isn't that what you're saying? I need six more months, is what I need. Enough time to finish the tapes."

"I can't promise that," Goodenough said. "I

84

can't offer you that. That is entirely out of my hands. If you go on this way, however, I do not think that you will have it."

Nothing else.

"Do you want me to stay?"

"To stay? To what?"

"To move in," Goodenough said. "Perhaps you would feel better if I were on the premises all the time. There is no reason why this could not be arranged. I could have a room—"

"You have other patients."

"Not any more."

"None?"

"Not for the time being. My sole role is to render you patient care. You are my only patient."

"You must think that I'm going to die soon," I said, "if you're willing to move in. You would only do that if you thought the end was near."

"I have never denied that," Goodenough said solemnly enough. "I have never tried to hold back from you the true facts of your condition."

"So you think the end is near?"

"At this rate, it is," he said.

"I'll fool you," I said. "I'll fool all of you. You're all waiting for me to die, but you're going to get a hell of a surprise. You're going to get a surprise like you've never had before in your life, because I am going to live and live. I am going to live for twelve or fifteen more years and bury all of you."

"Not if you keep on going this way."

"Get out," I said, "I don't want to talk to you anymore." I felt rage coursing through me, carried by the blood, rage palpitating the small and ruined cells of the heart. "I want you out of here now."

"Emotional lability," Goodenough said, standing. "These sudden switches, these inversions of

85

mood are characteristic of the condition, that's all. Don't you understand, Mr. President? You simply are no longer in control of yourself. This isn't you, it's the drugs talking. But it's too radical. It can't go on this way."

"Get out, you sanctimonious fuck," I said. "You sanctimonious old fuck and fool, get out of here. Get out of here now." I stood—quite a difficult operation, let me assure you. I will not describe it. It disgusts me to describe it. "Get out of here," I said.

Nothing resistant—he has never defied me in any form, way, shape or manner—Goodenough lumbered tangle-footed away from me, his bland features spreading open like a ripped heart, exposing the interior, softer, more dangerous flesh. "All right," he said, "I'll do that. I'll cooperate with you as I have from the first. But it's not working, don't you understand that? It's simply not working."

"I agree with you," I said, and of course I did. "I agree with you on that, but what's the alternative?" And he went out of there, leaving me alone with much to think about, I can assure you, except that thinking did not seem to be quite the course of action that I was looking for at the time. I went to the spools. Do not go gentle into those good spools but rage against the flickering of the recorder light.

Eunice died in 1981. It was a difficult occasion, of course; the question was, whether or not to go to the funeral. Although the divorce had been almost no issue at all during the campaign, had been pretty well covered over, as a matter of fact, by other issues, her death received pretty good play, and there was no question of sneaking into the funeral in a quiet and composed way. She died in the nursing home in which she had been bedridden for many years. She was only sixty-six years old, but from all the reports I was able to gather—and a President has fairly good intelligence when he puts his mind to it—she looked and acted much older; in fact, she had as advanced a case of senile dementia as a sixty-six-year-old woman is capable of having. The obituaries, however, cut off any discussion of her life after 1970, discreetly saying that she had retired from public activities. Her work in social welfare up until that time, however, had been well known. Eunice was always dedicated to social welfare, no more so than after I had left her.

"You're going to have to go," Hope said to me. One thing that lady could do was seize an issue. "It's going to be bad if you go, but it's going to be worse if you don't. So you might as well."

"She's no longer my wife," I said. She hadn't been my wife for almost a quarter of a century.

"That doesn't matter. You were married for almost eighteen years, you had a child, she was beside you all throughout your early career. You can't deny that kind of thing, Bill."

"I'm not denying it," I said, I thought reasonably enough, "there's nothing to deny. It just seems that it would force a feeling, a relationship that wasn't there."

"Bill," she said, "you're going to have to go because anything else would be worse"—she was right—"and the only way to make the best of it," she added, "is for me to go with you. If the two of us go, it will be somehow less personal, it will merely be a thoughtful, sincere gesture in which the two of us can join; whereas if you fail to go, or you go by yourself, everything may be raked up again. We couldn't have that, Bill."

What was there to say about the woman? Always her judgments were superior to mine, right up until the very end, when it could be said—although many may disagree—that her judgment was so great that it looked only like an enormous miscalculation, its true implications far removed from those like myself with more ordinary minds.

"All right," I said, "we'll handle it that way, even though it's going to turn it into something of a circus, don't you know that? Can't you see all of that coming?"

And if she was right about the one thing, then I was very distinctly right about the other; it was a circus—an affair of state is a more proper way to describe it. Eunice was buried in Omaha, where the nursing home was; there was no reason for her to be buried anywhere else. There was no other family, no one to particularly choose a site; the occasion created my going.

In the presidential jet we went there, with full presidential paraphernalia, five hundred at the funeral, all that could be admitted into the chapel, and another five thousand outside looking for a glance of the prince—the Prince of State if not the Prince of Sleep, that was. And looking at the bier, the closed coffin, I felt almost a lurch of feeling, something close to rage and loss intermingled in a way that had been very private to our relationship and which I had not thought of for twenty years—what the woman could evoke in me, what the woman could do to me. Hope must have seen this, the way I was locked into a small, silent, removed place far away from her.

At the end of the prayer and the brief eulogy by the head of the nursing home, telling about Eunice's great spirit and great optimism in her last days, I could really believe it. I felt myself, unbidden, lurching out of my feet, concerned servicemen snatching at my elbows. I waved them all away and staggered down the aisle, flashbulbs going off in funerary precision as I crossed the altar, leaned over and then past the coffin and ascended the stairs, then stood next to the head of the nursing home, who backed away from me, his eyes like that of a porpoise, and I said, "I would like to say a few words, if I might."

The minister said, "Surely." Some obscure Baptist on obscure assignment through the funeral home, they are a very special breed, these ministers.

"Just a few words," I said, as the minister, panicked, back-pedaled his way all the way off the podium and nearly into a pew, and gripped onto the lectern found myself regarding the mourners with an almost professorial stare, which was a horrible way to look at the situation. I could see the irony of it.

"I lived with this woman for many years," I said, "I was married to this woman. I have never denied her impact on my personality—her grace, her influence, the way in which she made almost every achievement of mine possible. This woman has suffered. She suffered two losses, a son in the flower of his youth to a terrible disease and the loss of a husband not many years later to something that she could only think of as another kind of terrible disease. And the two might have been interrelated; which is to say, how may one work on the other? But despite these two terrible shocks, this lady was able to go on, to live bravely and well, to move beyond her great and initial contributions to a different stage of life altogether in which her contributions were magnified and altered by being given to an ever larger body of people. As she had given to the one, so gave she to the many . . . and with those characteristics of grace, vision, and sacrifice which had been hers from the start."

It was a stirring speech, not the least bit affected by the fact that it was not so much felt as willed; I knew that she deserved better than she had gotten and this was an attempt, however weak, at reparations of some sort. The channels of the mind are devious and convoluted indeed if I thought that this constituted reparations; at any moment I could have swung my gaze into the open coffin where Eunice's eyes, dim and moist, cocked to alertness behind their half-closed lids, would have confronted me, could have looked up and down the angles of the corpse's body and felt an almost personal sense of revulsion for what had happened.

But I did not look at the open coffin, being very opposed to this kind of thing on principle, having already left the most explicit instructions in my own case that the coffin is to be closed at once and that discretion will abound throughout my own funeral. The deterioration of the aged in the flesh is quite enough; they are entitled to some privacy in their passage; age, senescence, corruption are public enough, the exhibition of enough shame ... let the lid be closed.

I said good-bye to Eunice in the most regretful and yet impersonal sense and stepped away from the podium to a great hush—it was a daring thing, of course, for a president (they said) to make a gesture of this sort and to rake over the ashes of a relationship which had long been thought to have been dangerous to his popularity. But then again (they said), he had long since been elected and had nothing to lose.

Leaving the chapel was the same panic as its entrance; for a moment I thought that I was going to be overwhelmed. This sensation was overtaking me more and more that year, that there was something uncontrollable about crowds and the nature of the public event, and that I would be whipped into a confrontation that I could not bear. . . . But we managed to get inside the limousine, the closed top one which Omaha had provided; and on the way to the airport, behind the shielding, Hope said, "You didn't feel a thing, did you?"

"I don't know," I said. "It had to be done."

"You didn't feel a thing," she said decisively, and her head nodded as if she were an auditor. "It was just something that you felt you ought to do."

"That's as good as feeling," I said. "If you do something because it ought to be done, and you do it right, what's the difference? The only thing that matters is the act."

"That's a very presidential statement."

"But it's true," I said, "isn't it true? Of course it's true; don't consider feelings, consider accom-

91

plishments. You want to know what happened, not how people felt when it was going on."

She shook her head. More and more that year she was moving away from me; I could not understand her. I had always found her accessible and comprehensible even if others did not, but since the election she had transmogrified into something else—was it First Ladyship itself that sat uneasily upon her? "I just hope you do better for me," she said, "I hope that you feel more."

"What? What's that?"

"I said, at my funeral I hope you have more feeling than you did at this one," she said, and then she said nothing at all. It was the first time she had ever done this to me—of course there were many other times as well, but one tends to remember the first—and as we whisked our way to the airport, it was with a feeling of all time coalescing, past and future telescoped into that one burning pass of her eyes as she looked at me, looked away from me, and left me there, hanging suspended by the threads of the thought of Eunice who was dead; and that was not the only death that year—oh, my, yes.

Inheriting the total cabinet, I thought it best to make the transition as inconspicuously as possible, to make as little of an alteration; but that was probably a serious mistake. Easy to know that now, but hard then, one's judgments always being superior in retrospect—this being part of the condition of being human. But it seemed best to retain the cabinet, to say nothing of the general structure of the executive branch, because my hold was so tenuous . . . or at least I thought it was tenuous. Like good Pope John I had been elected to tread water and to die. I think that many of them expected me to die in office, what with the curse; and with the question of age, it would have been the most equitable means of satisfying the curse, tossing the corpus into its maw, so to speak. Half-accepting that myself—the proposition, that is, that I would die in office (but quietly, not violently, something mild and exhilarating like a stroke that would black me out and send me on, spinning vault immediately), I hesitated to deal with the superstructure of the situation. It was simply better to go along—or so I thought.

Dolan could have helped me at that time, but Dolan had his own problems, suspended in a constant state of disbelief, vice-presidents not a species like thee and me but a special, private, sullen breed who can find communion perhaps only with one another. If I had worked with Dolan, there might have been more control; but Dolan, of course, was simply waiting for me to die in office along with the rest of them; and there was little possibility of connection, not that I wanted it. Everybody expected me to die in office. I should have known that the news magazines filled with speculations and hint; not a story I ever read in which my age was not mentioned first paragraph, last paragraph, and middle. And yet I went on, on and on with consummate stubbornness and grace; the aging or aged president of the United States went on—and what a surprise to them; what a surprise to Dolan as well as it seemed that I would, impossibly, beat all of the historical and mystical odds. But then again —and this was well remembered too—the curse applied to a second term as well. There was no reason why I should die in the first term. Lincoln hadn't; it was after reelection that he had been assassinated. It only held that presidents who were elected for the first time in years ending with zero would die in office, which gave me plenty of leeway; and there was the possibility, always the chance then, that I could beat it by standing aside at the last moment for reelection, resigning even ... I do not mean to imply that I was obsessed by this. Do not get the wrong impression.

Most of the time there was little thought given to it. A president can be a very busy man, after all, if he puts his mind to it; he can also be a very idle man—it all depends upon his personality. Johnson was busy, but Nixon did nothing; Kennedy was vigorous, but on the other hand my predecessor went off for long trapshooting sessions in the wilds of Tennessee and would not be heard of for weeks at a time—although a stream of releases, of course, gave an impression of vigor and dedication. This kind of thing can be arranged. The office has great potential for evasion of all sorts; one can evade as easily as one can confront, depending upon style—and certainly I did my evasions. But I did my confrontations as well, didn't I, doctor? Nothing ever was so far out of touch that I could not touch it; but then again nothing was ever near enough that I could not get away. The capacity of the office granted the occupant to move in and out alternately of situations is marvelous; it is almost sexual, wouldn't you say that, doctor? Oh, doctor, of

94

course, it would be sexual—moving in and out, out and in of situations, pumping them, milking them, exploding finally through them with a great dense fire . . .

Goodenough says that more radical action must be taken, but Goodenough does not truly understand the situation. I think Henry called him in; I think Henry and Goodenough are in collaboration to drive me insane. It was not time for his visit for a week and yet here he is, Goodenough, bag dangling from his wrists. "I warned you," he said, "I warned you that the effects would be increasingly temporary. You had a breakdown yesterday."

"I am going to finish," I said. "I am going to finish this project." My blood bubbled with steroids and radical cortisone therapy. I just learned that this morning, isn't that interesting? Radical and dangerous cortisone therapy, Goodenough perched way out on a limb not only for cause of his patient but for medical science as well. Steroids sang in my blood, bobbed up and down, bathed and laved one another, the effect of coming back into focus after having been out was almost orgasmic—not that anything down there is working at all; do not think that I have a dirty mind, doctor. "I will finish this project," I said, "my last great project. I am going to leave my memoirs, the true and final statement of my position. I am entitled to do this, and I will not stop as long as I have breath."

"You're going to kill yourself," Goodenough said to me. His face seemed translucent; I could see the carving of bone in some witchery of the light. "You are going to blow out with a hemorrhagic stroke." He stopped to take a deep breath, which neatly empurpled his complexion, and said, as if with great pride, "You nearly did yesterday, you know."

"Was that it? Was that what happened?"

Goodenough seemed to be beaming with some enormous secret inflating within him. "I won't go into it," he said. "There is no need to go into details of the situation. You know what is happening as well as I do. You were warned."

"I must finish," I said. I swung my aged, feeble gaze over the room, noticed that matters seemed out of perspective. I seemed to be peering as if from a reservoir. Looking around I could see enormous, swollen limbs rising. "You've got me strapped in!" I shrieked.

"Not at all," said Goodenough. My feathery struggles verified this; I was able to move from the waist up. "We've elevated your feet."

"What have you done to me?"

"We're trying to induce an opening up of the oxygen supply to the brain," Goodenough said. "Your feet are above your head." I could see that they were indeed suspended on massive pillows, seemingly floating. "It's a temporary prophylaxis. All of this is."

"I've got to finish," I said, allowing my feet to remain in their position. "Don't you understand? I've got to finish now."

"You're not doing very well," Goodenough said,

96

"it can't go on this way. Don't you understand? You're full of *cortisones* and *steroids* . . . this is a *very dangerous therapy*. And still you're not responding seriously. Your blood pressure is 280 over 120."

"You did this to me," I said. I felt possessed with mad conviction. The last throes of the aged are burlesque, all farce with pillows and tumbling. It is impossible not to see the humor of it, even the humor of what Goodenough has done to me, but the absence of dignity is insuperable. "I've got to finish, don't you see that?" My eyes must have been glaring madly. "Where's Merrick?" I said.

"Who?"

"Merrick. Isn't he on duty today?

Goodenough's eyes showed a faint understanding. "Oh," he said, "your attendant, you mean. He's off duty today."

"Where's Henry?

"Don't worry about that now."

"I want to talk to him."

"You're not in any condition to talk to anyone. You'd better lay back right now." Goodenough seemed to be oozing excitement or then again maybe it was only perspiration. "Everything's failed," he said, as if he was announcing some profound medical discovery, "and the risk factor is too great. I think we're going to have to institutionalize."

"No," I said.

"You intend to go on this way?"

"Then move in with me. If that's the only answer, then you can do that. I'll let you stay."

Goodenough shook his head. "You misunderstand. You've always misunderstood. I don't want to move in with you. I offered it before as a last resort. But you didn't want it. You rejected it then and I think that you're right to reject it now. It's too far advanced."

"No," I said. It seemed to be the only word left in vocabulary, or then again perhaps in the manner of the aged I had made the negative affirmative. It is not easy to say. Everything is irretrievably complex. "I must finish. I only have a little further to go."

"What is the point of this?" Goodenough said. "What does it matter whether or not you get these down?"

"It matters to me. Don't you understand that? What could be more important? These are the true and final recollections of my administration."

"It is my duty to regard this only from the medical standpoint. From the medical standpoint, this cannot be considered within the elements of acceptable risk. Cortisones and steroids have unimaginable side effects, and the further we go in trying to strike a balance, the more radical the symptomatology. Haven't you seen that?"

"Increase the dosage."

"You're on massive doses already. We've already exceeded all tolerable limits."

"Increase them," I said. I waved my feet in the air, the wriggling of the toes like beacons from another aspect of space. "Increase them all you want. Move in with me. Give me a constant monitor."

"This is insane," Goodenough said, but he shook his head, and from his eyes a little perceptive light gleamed. He must have seen it as a great and final challenge, the great and final challenge of his life, just as I did. We find our purposes, our

98

great accomplishments in the strangest places. "It increases the risk factor unacceptably, I told you. God, how far could we push it?"

"Try."

"It would be impossible."

"You could write a paper," I said. "You'd be famous. You're famous already, the president's physician. Think of that abstract in preparation! Think of what it would mean if you could test the limits of the treatment."

"My obligation is to keep my patient alive. It is not to see how far I can go to kill a patient."

"That's my decision."

"Why do you want to die?" Goodenough said, and I looked back at him. There was no need really to say anything; and to his credit, his face softened from its inquisitive glare. "All right," he said, "no one can stop you. If you want to do this, you could find someone easily enough who would help you if I refused. So it might as well be someone who has your interests at heart."

"Right. That's right."

"You'll have to keep your feet elevated all the time. That increases the blood supply to the brain."

"I like to talk and move about at the same time. I think better when I'm moving about."

"We can give you some elastic stockings. Tight elastic stockings. They will constrict the blood vessels below and increase the supply of oxygenated blood to the brain. But they're going to be very painful."

"Old women wear elastic stockings."

"You're asking me to help you," Goodenough said. "I'll try to help you. But you must follow instruction. We're not considering the cosmetic aspects here."

"I was just joking."

"If we can keep your feet elevated and have heavy constriction and increase the cortisones and steroids a little further because of the immobilization, we might buy a little time. The end is going to be catastrophic, however."

"The end is always catastrophic. Tell me when it is not a disaster. When was death ever otherwise?"

"I'm being very frank with you. I hope you appreciate that I'm being honest with you. I've never tried to conceal—"

"I know, doctor," I said. "You've told me that before. It's very much appreciated. I can't tell you how much I appreciate your frankness and medical honesty," I said and peered at him through the little aperture of self, the thin line of sight that was permitted me in this position, and saw him in a way that I never had before, his face riven by emotion—or then again I only may have been imagining this—some cast of feeling to the face which I would never have apprehended before. It was too much for me—oh, too much for me indeed—cortisones and steroids roiled sickeningly in the ruined circulation, blown through the diminishing pump of self. And I felt myself falling away from there through some dilating tunnel of sensation, but knew as always before that I could never fall so far away but that I would not be back there again, see the light again, cut my way through those ruined spokes of light once more—and those broken spokes were America itself.

"I've made my decision," I said to him. "The question is, have you made yours?"

"Talk, you old fart," he said, "you old son of a bitch, do you want to blow up—"

"But yes," I said, "don't you understand that?" I turned toward him. I missed Dolan at that moment; it would have been a good thing to have had an audience. I would have appreciated an audience if only to measure the reactions, because they were too profound and complex to be wasted on one person—me, who was himself a participant. "I want you to tell me how it feels. What it's like to have on your conscience what you're going to do? Because I'm going to call the bluff," I said. "I'm going to let you people go ahead and have your cities. Your demands are impossible. They are, as a matter of fact, suicidal." I went to the intercom and picked up the phone. I ordered the Secret Service in and hung up the phone. "We're going to put you under arrest."

"You'll never get away with this. You'll never—"

"The situation can't be saved," I said. "You've already blown up two installations. You've given us no room for manuever at all, you see. Maybe the next time, you'll learn something about politics, something that any state assemblyman could have told you. Don't box your opponent in. Don't spring your worst before you've even given him a chance to negotiate. Once you do that, once you

101

carry out your threat without giving the threat itself a chance to work, then you've left your opponent with no room at all because you've offered him nothing. You've already done the worst. You could have worked something out, you were in a very good position; the infiltration was cleverly arranged, you've planned this for a year, and the takeover was excellent. You caught us flat-footed. It was inconceivable that these plants would be overtaken by saboteurs. But you've left us with nothing, and you've left yourself with nothing. Two installations gone is so bad that you might as well go three and four."

"Man," he said, "man, you're crazy." His eyes were wild. I mean his eyes were rolling and flickering within his face; I had never seen them so out of control in a human being. At the end, leaning over Arthur's bedside, seeing what the drugs were doing to him, seeing the creeping patterns in the network of the blood as they had rolled and surfaced to his eyes, I might have seen something like this; but what lay shrouded behind Arthur's pupils was different from what I saw here. The man began to convulse. His body slammed against one of the walls, he jackknifed, moved in against himself, collapsed to the floor. I thought it was an epileptic fit. The Service was in the room. They looked at him on the floor. He coiled and uncoiled as if to mark the passage of electricity.

"Get him out of here," I said. They looked at me wonderingly. "Arrest him." Are you sure you want to do this? their glances said. "Get him out of here," I said, "put him through the legal processes; I'll have nothing more to do with him." Have you considered the consequences? their ex-

102

pressions said. "I've considered everything. I don't care." He was still writing on the floor. "Get him out of here before he vomits," I said, and they dragged him out. Presidential orders are presidential orders, regardless of the condition of the executive, Nixon having proved that; and in the office, again alone, I had to think very little before I issued the orders that had to be—and then there was nothing to do but wait.

They threatened to tear up Boulder, but nothing happened. The militia went into that plant and got them all without a struggle. In Cleveland they surrendered at White Sands; there was a little bit of a fire fight, but nothing explosive. After White Sands the rest of them came out voluntarily. Fallout was contained within the narrowest perimeter; they had worked out clean fusion.

The situation was saved. I was a national hero. What a great outpouring of love! It was only Hope who knew, and how could it have been concealed from her? How did I think she would not know, that I had done all of it from weakness? They had left me simply nothing else to do at all.

I had not been lying to the man.

They had simply left us without any room at all for negotiation. If they had, I would have capitulated. I would have given up the office itself if there had been room for manuever. But there was none at all. I struck out, cornered, in terror.

Lying here, the elasticity of the stockings binding tightly around ankles and calves, sending (Goodenough insists) revivifying little jolts of blood to the brain, I have encountered an entirely new way of looking at reality or that simulacrum of reality which is my operating terrain these days; there is no question but that on the one hand, as Goodenough has predicted, the cortisone and steroids, along with the elasticity and elevation, have put me back into relative contact. I feel far more lucid and able to rake through the garden of the past patiently than I have for quite a time, and it is possible closing my eyes at times to find such an astonishment of recall, such a pinpoint precision of recollection that I can describe every object in the room . . . this is not the action of an eighty-year-old man.

I feel revivified, a hoarse, hysterical seventy at least, seventy-five anyway . . . but on the other hand, staring at existence through supp-hose socks, as spied through the lump made by the cannister strapped to my thigh, my head some three feet below the level of the feet on this very strange contrivance they have rigged for me, this parody of a bed . . . this is no picnic at all. I feel that I have lost that fundamental control over the situation which was always the key to my ability to confront reality—that I could control it. Lying back here in swooning ease, babbling my reminiscences into this microphone held not two inches from my lips, little flecks of phlegm and drool mingling on the holes so that now and then I must put out an indolent thumb, wipe them away, this is not contrived to give one that internal sense of dignity from which placidity and true, reasoned recall must issue.

Then too I have lost Merrick, for reasons that cannot be explained—not Henry, Henry remains with me, although of a rather more mournful temper; it must be his friend that he is missing. But Merrick is gone from me and has been replaced by a lady in a white uniform who tells me that she is to be called Margaret and that she will tend to me. She and Doctor Goodenough are in the closest of consultation, and what he tells her and she in turn tells me can be considered direct orders. Margaret will brook little or no nonsense; she is a shapeless woman defined merely by the uniform but to see her merely in her role as a trained nurse—I suspect that this is what she is, a trained nurse—would be to misunderstand the situation; she is every bit as much of a personality as the departed Merrick, the sullen Henry, and her interest in me is not at all clinical—is that not right, Margaret? She has just come into the room. The woman will not leave me alone, unlike Merrick or Henry, who would disappear for long convivial periods in the pantry or the adjacent rooms, doubtless drinking and exchanging reminiscences of other patients—they have known famous and obscure—unlike these two gentlemen, who combined forbearance with inarticulateness, with understanding, in a way which reminded me of a postmaster general in those dear, departed days before the office had been abolished . . . unlike those people, Margaret is dedicated to her work—isn't that right, Margaret? She takes it seriously and personally and is constantly fluffing, pulling, arranging, supporting, kneading, rubbing, administering, whispering; the woman is driving me out my fucking mind—not that I realize it is for the best, my dear—and she has never interrupted me. Yet even when I say the most shocking and disgusting fucking shitty motherfucking shitty phallic things into this microphone, does she even give me a twitch of an eyelash. You are a miracle, Margaret.

A miracle, Margaret, you remind me of my first wife, you old cunt. Have I told you about my first wife? Well, it is all on the tape now. Supporting my back on pillows, thrusting up and into her, I would feel as she came down in counterweight that it was not so much the activity as the sheer *weight* of her which would destroy me, not that she was a heavy woman, but the expression of disapproval, her breasts flying like pillows, the dry, hard, metallic sheath of her cunt colliding against me as she would move up and down, everything poised as it were toward a revulsion so profound that it was private, immutable . . . all of this, Margaret, gave me the feeling that with every downward thrust, every bitter curve in her mouth, she was willing me toward annihilation. She made me feel so *guilty*—that is what I am trying to say.

Back in those days, in the twenties, I mean, we were hardly raised to regard sex as if it were the most guiltless of passions; but even for that era, Eunice was something remarkable. I don't think the woman enjoyed it once. I can never recall her showing any sensation other than forbearance, and she would never out of the bed refer to it— not once in retrospect. She would not even admit that it existed between us; it was just something dirty and subterranean which occurred in that tiny enclosure of the sheets, and was otherwise negligible, beneath negligibility; it was something that was an object of revulsion, except that revul-

sion demanded thought, and she did not have any
of that either. Am I making this clear?

I think then that she blamed herself for Arthur
—Arthur's cancer, that is. She had a theory that
the way the child was conceived was the key to the
personality and physique of the child; that if a
child were conceived in love, the child would be a
strong, loving individual; but it it were conceived
in hatred or in indifference, those limitations
would show within the child's very expression, the
life which it adopted. . . . You are asking me,
Margaret, I am sure, how she could reconcile this
theory with her own hatred for sex. And I can
only tell you that in her own mind, she surely believed that she loved me very much; and if she
had not, she would not have been able to participate in sex at all—that was her rationalization. . . .
But when Arthur got the first diagnosis, all of
that fell away, and I saw her face as it had been
in the bed twenty-two years before, desperate,
caved in, the eyes hollow and bleak, staring outward, staring inward, fixated on nothing whatsoever.

He died eight months after the final diagnosis;
that is remarkable, I understand—usually they go
in four or five months, and the most heroic efforts
rarely get them beyond six. But he held on for a
full eight months and twelve days, dwindling within himself all of the time but in contact until the
very end. And as his body became more and more
compressed, so did it seem to shrink into a point
of hardness; there was less of the flesh, but the
spirit remained the same, so as the corpus sprang
tighter around Arthur, there was more of him
peeping out inertly through the windows of his
entrapment; and all of the time as he shrank and

dwindled, so did his intensity increase. At the very end he was all purpose, concentrated, bleak, and staring on the bed. If I went up, Arthur came down—or so I thought in those days, but my thinking was not characterized by any unusual lucidity.

It was difficult enough to deal with Eunice, who I had not seen at all in five years but whose relationship I had to painfully reconstruct over and over again in the times when I went to the hospital (which was often enough, but not enough to suit me). She blamed me for everything, of course. If I had not left her, Arthur would not have gotten leukemia. If our marriage had lasted, our son would have lasted. If there had not been something corrupt, rotten, and sick about our marriage, then our son would have been strong, healthy, and wise.

He served in the Peace Corps in Uganda, you know; I think it was the only thing in life that he ever wanted to do, the only time that he was actually doing something which was his, rather than contrived for him; but that ended pretty fast. They sent him home sick, and he went to the hospital immediately. At least Eunice never blamed Kennedy or the Peace Corps for that. It would have opened up fascinating levels of material—perhaps more than I could have handled—if she had taken that aspect on it, but she never did.

Finally he died. He died three days before Kennedy was killed, and although the collision of events was momentarily shocking, it was probably the best thing that could have happened to Eunice or myself—not that I want to turn that dreadful public event into anything reflecting personal gain—but it did . . . Arthur died; Kennedy was killed; Oswald was killed. It became apparent that we were living in a universe whose insanity was not circumscribed but which rather leached over into the lives and circumstances of others, so one could not conceive of a personal or malevolent destiny; it was general. The insanity was malignant, all right, but at least it could be said that it was not particular; it chose no favorites; it got all of us. I think it was this knowledge that wheeled Eunice around.

Certainly there was no extended period of mourning. For me, there was enough to do in those days after the assassination to make the thought of personal loss somehow irrelevant— great tasks, great deeds, we were putting a nation together . . . I did not think of the curse then. It was only some months later that talk about the curse began to filter its way into the circuits of discussion, and then only in an idle and abstract way. It was generally thought that the Kennedys had such particular bad luck that they did not need the curse to explain what had happened to them. Nevertheless, over the years I thought about it. Certainly all of us did. It was one of those undercurrents washing the national psyche, along with so much else.

Arthur died. He had not been conceived in love, but this is not to say that he was conceived merely in lust either; he was conceived the way most people are, that is to say, out of a kind of tropism. I believe that I am going to vomit, Margaret. This is something that has not happened before. You had better get this microphone out of my hand before I do something . . .

The Hope Diamond, curse and all, has been the property of the United States of America, courtesy of the Smithsonian Institution, since sometime in the late 1950s. I wonder if anybody has ever considered this.

"I don't want to run again," I told Hope. "I think this decision is irrevocable."

"Don't be ridiculous," she said, "we've had this discussion before. There hasn't been a morning since the election when you haven't complained and complained, but you know perfectly well that you're going to do it; this is your obligation, and furthermore you've never been happier. You're going to be renominated and reelected and serve four more years and finish your work."

"What work?" I asked. "What work are you talking about? There is no work. It is merely a matter of filling in time. And if I do it this way, the way you suggest, I'll be seventy-eight years old in my last year of office. Seventy-eight years old—that's ridiculous. That's no age for a president. And what kind of retirement can I look forward to? No, I really don't want to run. I am quite serious about this. I think I am going to make a statement next week."

"You're not going to make any statement," she said. She liked being First Lady more than I liked being president. This is not an exceptional observation, of course; it would apply to almost all First Ladies and every president. "You are going to be renominated and reelected because you are the best man for the job and you owe it to the country."

"Seventy-eight years old? I'm going to be seventy-eight years old in the last year and I owe this to the country."

"De Gaulle was seventy-eight years old and still premier," she said. "Churchill was seventy-eight years old."

"And look what happened to them."

"You think it makes any difference?" she said. "Everybody gets old and senile, everybody dies. It's a question of how you spend your life."

"I don't want to spend my life this way," I said. "There must be some other way to spend my life. I want to go fishing."

Both of my wives were very determined women. Both of my wives knew exactly what was the best thing for me to do, the most moral and courageous action; the fact that it just happened to be to their best advantage as well was merely coincidence. They would not have thought for the moment of doing anything that was not for my best interests. If I had reconstructed Eunice with Hope, then perhaps I had anticipated Hope with Eunice.

Is the future a reenactment of the past? Or can we say that what we are merely comes from the dark anticipation of what we will be? This is a question which I meant to ponder sometime before the very end, but it is obviously too late for that now, and it might be better to stick to the main topic of discussion. I did not want to run again.

"Who's going to try and stop you?" Hope said. "Why, it's impossible for anyone to win this election for the party except you, and you owe it to the party." And then she walked away from me. She was always doing that you know, preparing incisive, devastating lines and then deserting a conversation. Maybe the lines were not so incisive or devastating, but there is nothing like a quick exit to give them color and density beyond perhaps what they really deserve. Owe it to the party! Why, I did not! Owe it to myself; I had no obligation whatsoever.

But the struggle over the nuclear power plants was still holding a year later. The outburst of popularity and love for my "courage" and "forbearance" and "strength" showed no signs of declining. Why, from the way it looked on the charts, you would have thought those two cities that were half-pulverized were filled with saboteurs instead of citizens and that in essentially being party to their ruin (for I was nothing else), I had been a martyr.

It is impossible to figure the complexities of politics. Mostly I left it to staff. After Nixon it was easy to leave it with staff, I mean, although I was never so much above the battle as I pretended to be. No president is, to be sure. "Above the battle." "Pretended to be." Hobbling and limping, stumbling and scurrying, cannister banging on my thigh, I will make my way yet into the plains of cliché before Goodenough, his steroids, and their cortisones are done with me. Cliché is irresistible. We could hardly live without it framing all of the dimensions of our lives.

The situation was good and the charts encouraging; however; I would hardly have walked away from it without ample consideration. No one but a fool walks away from that; most of us have to be carried, even at the mandatory end, out of it—consider Johnson. Still as that smudged and equivocal year of 1984 staggered on, as my luck held, as the curse stayed in abeyance, that small blooming shoot of a thought which had been little more than an apprehension years before poked its irresistible way under the surfaces of the brain more and more the semaphore of consciousness: by God, I might just get away with it. I had much less than a year to go. If I refused renomination and actually managed to see a successor inaugurated, then I would have the curse beaten and at the age of seventy-four, would be able to enjoy the fullness and opportunities of life available to a seventy-four year old.

I would have gotten out of it clean, which is something that could not be said of any of us after Eisenhower—and how clean can Eisenhower be said to have been? I knew that dark old man a little bit in the middle years of his retirement, and all of his equanimity can be said to have been ceremonial. This would have been something new for me then, if I had been able to bring it off, but there were so many pressures—pressures not only from Hope (who was unofficial cultural affairs commissioner and who loved her work) but from the party itself. Doddering as I might have been, I was still washed by national approbation and was, to be sure, the only absolute winner that the party could nominate.

Also, I must concede myself, that there are pleasant aspects to the presidency of the United States: one is insulated at all levels from woe or worry; one has any number of personal prerogatives satisfied; and for one who does not travel— as was my policy never to go out of the country, dedicating my administration to the recognition and solution of painful national problems—it can be considered to be an extended if rather pressured vacation at the highest levels of luxury. . . . Any President who tells you that it is not essentially fun is lying; all of Johnson's crabbing and bitching about loneliness and decision-making was so that they wouldn't get wise to him and throw him out. It is one of those offices, in short, from which it is almost impossible to resign; one must be thrown out—or as in the case of constitutional guarantees, mandated out.

As we plunged toward the summer of '84, insulated as I was, I felt the pressures mounting, balanced off against that the little frail shoot of a flower of possibility was as nothing, only fit to be trampled . . . and yet within me a secret was buzzing greedily, for all of it was counterfeit. I knew this; everything had been contrived on a single misapprehension underlying the nuclear blackmail, and no one understood this. I did not want it to be understood, of course, but on the other hand, it is not pleasant living a basic deceit —oh, you can understand my conflicts, my pain, my doubt, my indecision. Conflict may be the most important element of the satisfactory novel and by implication may also be the key to the success of these memoirs, the second serial rights to

114

which I hope to sell to all of the important newspapers via the press syndicates to say nothing of the movie rights (there is certainly a hell of a movie in my life, is there not?) and I have contrived them toward that end. The conflict was within, not without: I knew something which none of them knew and which I would not dare to tell, cannot tell at this moment, the real reason why I stood up to the blackmailers and dared them to annihilate the millions. Oh the burning of the brain, folks, the merry, tarry burning of the brain, small drops of the horrid jelly dripping, dripping like scepters in the night of the light of the skull.

"Here," she says. "Here is today's therapy." Goodenough stands behind her, beaming. He has never looked better. He is carrying equipment and a smile lightly; aglow and alert within his responsibility. "Do take it," she says, extending her hand on which I see a light, bright pill.

"No," I say. The pill casts back colors that I have never seen before. "I do not want to."

"You must."

"I will not," I say. "I am entitled to the integrity of my prophylaxis. Besides, I am getting stronger. Every day in every way and my memoirs are coming along."

"If you do not take it," she says, her hand steady, giving me what must be even to her internal monitors a rather horrid smile. Every given expression of her is a rather horrid smile. "If you don't take it, we're going to have to go to more radical theory."

"What is it?" I say.

"This is a vasal dilator," Goodenough says. "It will open up certain passageways and reduce arterial blockage."

"I've never seen a pill like that," I said. I had swallowed unthinkingly everything that had been placed before me, had rotated myself benignly for every shot in anal or deltoid area, had turned myself upon the spit of a circumstance; like a patient, overpaid whore, I had accepted everything that was given unto me, but something about the size of the pill made me resist. It was orange. And as I peered closely, I could see upon it the shadow outlines of imprinting, some marks as if in another tongue, which for all I knew might have been obscenities. It would have been all the same. I did not know. "No," I said. I dug my old, gnarled hands into the smooth and slippery surfaces of the couch on which I was reclining heavily, retracted my head like a passenger slinking back into the receptors of an automobile. "No," I said again.

Goodenough held the pill, Margaret closing ground behind him, holding a glass of water, the two of them staring at me as if they were parents in some hideous parody of the primal scene, the pill objectification of that subtle exchange working between them. They could have been my mother and father, I thought, and of course the likelihood of the image sprung into my mind. It was proper that I would think of them that way because senility is the true and final passage, the absolute circularity of life, closing the gap, so they had become my parents. I was completely enthralled to them; they could do anything that they wanted to me, little stabs of paranoia like illness flickering up and down.

"No," I said again; it was the first resistance I had ever shown any of their medications. I was surprised myself at the force of my denial; I would not have thought that there was so much revulsion in me. "No, I won't take that. You can't do it to me."

And with a lurch Goodenough came toward me, closing the space, his palm opened like a priest's, dispensing blessing, and the pill fell into my mouth like a wafer, glowing briefly in the drop, then falling between teeth and tongue, my mouth still hanging open in protest, and I choked. Goodenough smiled; a beam came from one side of his face to the other in a transfigurative way, and he moved aside as Margaret took the cup of water, inserted it in my mouth, and forced me to take choking swallows—it was either that or inhale the water. I felt pill and water sealing together in some obscure way within the cave of self, and then, as if it were music, I felt a slow, murmuring, billowing within. I inhaled slowly, trying to pace out the breaths. The sensations were excruciating.

"I told you this would help," Goodenough said.

"Don't you feel better now?" said Margaret.

"This is going to oxygenate you; it's going to give you some of that oxygen which the constriction has cut off. You'll be able to think again. You'll find that your mental processes return toward alertness."

"You'll think much better," Margaret said. "This is good for you; it's going to make everything seem so much easier—"

"Of course, the effect is temporary," Goodenough said. "All of the effects are always temporary. But there's reason to be exceedingly optimistic about this."

"Don't you feel better?" Margaret said and put a hand on my palpating, twitching brow. "Of course you feel better; I think that fever's going already. You're getting a nice, nourishing supply—"

"And of course those memoirs will go along fine now," Goodenough said. "You'll find that your energy levels are much higher, that you'll be able to concentrate for longer periods, and that they won't get away from you the way that you might have been afraid they were doing. I think that this is the right step."

"Oh, definitely," Margaret said, "definitely this is the right step." Her hand did not desist nor did her pressure upon my brow. "You go right ahead, Mr. President, you go right ahead now and work."

"I warned you of the risk factor," Goodenough said. "We were always very honest to you, but within the risk factor—"

"Oh, yes," Margaret said, "oh, yes, there's always risk; life is risk, isn't that the truth, sweetie? But you're doing much better, you're doing so much better—"

And falling back on the couch then, I saw another aspect of the truth or as close to the truth as I might come; that at the end it would be as the beginning, and that these furies chanting over me were neither priests nor predators, neither fiends nor salvation but only those versions of the primal scene which I had myself glimpsed—and as I came, so I would return, all of the sounds coming over me for the first time in years. I felt growing

118

above the place where the cannister was set a palpable erection, not quite an exclamation point but a comma, at least some little breathing strophe in the rivers which plunged toward darkness.

But difficult to concentrate, focus, they were right, the mind churning in wild activity, so many thoughts—I have never had so many *thoughts*. But the microphone is holding me down, my hand is holding me down, my voice is holding me down, the sheer need for language to sit here patiently and speak into the microphone chains me, I do not have the patience to sit and talk, rather I want to run wildly over the room.

Closing my eyes I can see my actions run at one-and-one-quarter speed, like the old films; clownishly I race through the room, toppling unsettling things, materials falling in slow motion just as I move in quicktime. I want to explode with activity, move chattering out of these rooms in search of companions or auditors. I could make a campaign speech in this mood or some declaration of conscience for the nation; impossible to lie here, my huge clownish feet suspended above me; all I need is buttons on the shoes and bell-bottoms, a red and glaring nose, wink and cast in the eye.

I could hurl this microphone across the room and catch it on the fly—but am locked here in place. Damn it! Straps here, straps there, huge pillows propping up the feet, and the shoulders way down in the couch impossible to move, cannot even roll; they have put me in position where I cannot move but the mind raving and wandering free.

Is it possible that they are preparing me for exhibition? I could see that. I could see the doors flicking open at a certain point and the press pouring in, all of them, first interview the president has given in two years, first time the president has made public appearance since the last inauguration. How are you, Mr. President? Oh, yes, I could see that. Answering from the muffled depths of my pillow, I'm just fine. Do you have any statement, Mr. President? Not at the present time. How has your retirement been? How have your memoirs been progressing? Well, it is very difficult to answer that in a sentence satisfactorily, I suppose. A picture, Mr. President? No, I'd prefer that no pictures be taken. Don't be modest, sir, and the explosion of light in the room, the pictures coming out the next day . . . I would have to confront my own appearance, something which I have not had to do in a considerable length of time. I do not think that I am ready for this; I do not think that I have reached the point where I am really able to look at a photograph of myself, much less deal with a public appearance. But they are undoubtedly preparing me for that.

Paranoia now streaks in coloration; I am positive that they are out to get me. They would be utter fools if they were not. I am sure that if I were in Goodenough's position, I would do the same. I would sell out to the press. I would take advantage of my position.

Still spewing out my memoirs, trying to make

120

some sense of it, the reels stacked up one by one on the shelf above me to the right near the door; and it is only faith that all of those memoirs lie stacked up here. First Merrick, then Henry, now Margaret pick up the completed spools from the recorder and they add them to the shelf. But there is no way of knowing when I am sleeping in the unseen enclosure of the night whether or not they may not be playing with these reels, feeding them through the recorder, mapping out my laborious reminiscences . . . how do I know that they are not listening to them, playing with them, making sport of this my life's work, perhaps even sending out the reels to an anxious set of institutions and substituting them with blanks?

I have thought of this from time to time. I am taking so much on faith; the confidentiality of my babblings is something in which I must believe in order to maintain that essential sense of control which enables the great work to go on, and yet there is no basis on which I can be sure of this. I know nothing. I have no assurance whatsoever that what I think is on that shelf is truly lying there. I know the recorder works because occasionally I engage in playback listening to the (always shocking, I did not know I sounded that bad) sounds of my voice; but as far as the project itself . . . I have no assurance. None whatsoever.

Still, what is the difference? At all costs I must go on; it would make no difference whether or not there was integrity to the reels; I would continue. What else do I have? Besides, when I get the full and final explication down on tape, I know that I could die in peace—which would be the only framing point and purpose to all of this, the only referent I can possess . . . if these memoirs cannot be punctuated by death, what veracity will they have? Obviously it is that rounding and final symbol which I desire.

But I do not know; I do not know about the integrity of the project. I dream sometimes in the clinging night that they are sitting there, Goodenough, Henry, Margaret, the unseen attendants of the night, and that they are listening to these reels, the playback of a day's ravings. Sometimes Margaret twitches or coughs; she is instantly motioned to silence by a furious Goodenough, who is bent over the machine, his features contorted with concentration. Sometimes Henry sneezes, a long, riffling bark of sound, the sneeze trailing off into a whimper, the way that the cries of orgasm are likely to do; and Goodenough turns that furious gaze upon him again, the eyes bland and bovine in the face, curiously expressionless even as he urges Henry to silence. Now and then one of the attendants giggles as something obscene comes off the tapes, instantly silencing himself; Margaret bends forward, lets out a fart like the sound from a cannon; Goodenough pokes a finger into his ear, begins to wring out wax and fluids while with his other hand he continues to take desperate notes, the pen rattling across the paper, while all of them suck on cigarettes, devour drinks, whisper to one another hurriedly in the pauses. But all through this the tapes drone on. Nothing can stop them but that they are heard through to the end; with fascination, my grisly little set of auditors incline their heads toward them. Buried on those tapes they feel is some fragment of knowledge, some delicate epiphany which will yank them around and frame the entire sense of their lives. No less than me, they are looking for some meaning to come out of those tapes, and they dare not miss a word lest they miss epiphany . . . but though they hush one another, though they pass notes back and forth, though Goodenough distends his mouth to great yawns of speculation now and then, they hear nothing. The tapes do not give them what they want.

Disappointed in the dawn's early light, the last shrinking spool clattering tape out of its twin, they are in the task of cleaning up. No one must know how they have spent their night. I must not deduce their purposes; if I did, I would feel constraint in my dictation, possibly would cease in my conversation, and where would they be then? Well, they would be nowhere at all; that is the answer. They would be unable to continue their search. So with hushes and cautions uttered through pursed lips, they begin the laborious task of cleaning up so that the room is in the same state of filth and disorder that it was when I left it: here an empty glass, there a discarded bottle, little strips of toilet tissue replaced, boxes in which the stockings came strewn throughout the room . . . not for a moment would I know that anyone had been there, that my tapes were being casually, carefully audited in the night. They are careful about this, there is nothing lackadaisical about their efforts to leave everything as it was. But despite their cleverness, despite all of their admonitions, I can tell; and come night after night, barking and yapping from the kennel of sleep, snaffling like a dog into the pillow . . . deep in dreams I must know all of this, must be one of the auditors in that room, my kindly, ponderous spirit lurking around them, my great, bearlike head nodding its own rhythms of assent; my spirit is truly then and all around them. And by the time I am taken from the bed, assisted through the task of dressing like a child, led into the bathroom to evacuate the remnants of my bowels, and plopped into the couch in my state of risen feet, I am already exhausted, not so much from the efforts of the morning, which are grim enough, but from all of the attentions squandered through the night. . . . I have missed none of it; I am on both shifts; I am dictating during the day and listening at night, just as they are listening through the night and administering to me during the day, an exhausting and pointless cycle for all of us. I wish that it could stop . . . but that would mean the taping itself would have to stop, and this is obviously impossible. I will not hear of it.

Campaigning: from Fargo to New Orleans to Mobile to Dallas within twelve hours, seeing nothing but the interiors of the plane, the limousine, the hotel rooms, and the television studios into which I am guided. To campaign is no longer to see the country—that is understood—but only to see the interior of various enclosures; pointless to attend a rally which attracts ten thousand people, several of whom might be potential assassins, when for one-half the cost and one-tenth the effort, one can make a taping in a local studio which will be shown on the metropolitan network reaching two million base audience on the six o'clock news; pointless to shake hands, whatever mystical strength may be drawn from the crowd, the hand squeezed to pulp when one can instead meet a selected group of citizens at an informal cocktail gathering, all of it being filmed for the eleven o'clock, a bank of local and national reporters tracking all of this. The travel then is merely for the effects, the brief splices on the newscast showing one disembarking or embarking once again, the personal appeal, that is to say, but the only personal appeal is into the eye of that cranking camera.

And deep into the summer of 1980, the polls indicating that it was going to hold, the slender consensus was going to hold and unless I did something disastrous I would be president. I said to Hope, "We are not seeing the country. We are not dealing with the people. We are merely going from room to room. We came not to listen but to talk."

"What's wrong with that?" she said. She was optimistic until the last. She really loved politics; that must be understood. I will give her credit for that. "It's what people want."

"But we're just talking; we're not listening," I said. "I don't think anyone's listened for years. That may be the reason for most of the real trouble in the country—nobody knows what's going on. I don't know what's going on, and I'm running for president."

She shook her head. "I can never stand you when you become idealistic or ironic or cynical or groping," she said. "There's nothing more boring than a politician talking about metaphysics. For God's sake, you know you love it, you know that this is what you do best. Why do you have to make yourself hate it? There's nothing wrong with any of this. Let's have sex," she said. She put herself down on the bed and hitched her skirt up.

"Sex now?" I said. "For God's sake, the press is supposed to be up here in five minutes and there's a conference—"

"Right now," she said. I do not know if her look was mischievous or passionate—maybe a little of both, maybe neither. I could never tell. I could never tell with her; her moods were always veiled. She was always coming at me on at least two levels, so at no point, even in the most intimate or perilous moments, did I know how she was feeling, what was the constituent of her thought. Even her cries in orgasm seemed to have a willed quality, but then again it is difficult to say exactly what she was willing.

"It's ridiculous," I said, and yet my seventy-year-old prick was already squirming within my seven-day-old suit. It is a shameful thing for me to remember how I used to be sexually, right up until 1986—or maybe it was seven; I was always able to do *something*. I could even give myself erections just thinking about it and—fool that I was—thought this was somehow shameful or disgraceful, certainly not presidential. Of course, she was twenty years younger than me, this must be remembered. It is something to keep up with a younger woman; it will either kill you or revive you. In my case it did both.

"Come on," she said, her elegant face appearing at angle between her legs. With the skirt pulled all the way up, her face was now peering at me through her crotch. The juxtaposition of

126

pubic hair glinting through her panties and the cool, graciousness of her face was exciting—like looking through a peephole in a Victorian bathroom to see a Princess diddling herself. "Come on," she said again, yanking down her panties, "you don't have to undress or anything, just unzipper and take it out."

"Ridiculous," I said, "what if they find us?"

"Isn't the door locked?" she asked.

"Well," I said, "it's locked but even so—"

"Then what?" she said. "What's the difference; what can happen if they come in the middle? *You* can come in the middle. Will you stop manufacturing excuses, Bill?"

It was madness. This was New Orleans (I believe in one of the Sheratons), not that there was any sense of place that summer, but for the record it was New Orleans. I got on top of her, a few fragile pumps and I was able to make an insertion and connection, then rocking easily above her, running my hands over the cloth of her dress.

"You are a pretty agile seventy year old," she said. Even then she had begun mocking me about my age. All of that had started somewhere in the previous year; until then she had never mentioned it, never mentioned the gap. "For a seventy-year-old man you are fantastic," she added, her cunt like a hand gripping me then and beginning to yank me forward. "Oh, Mr. President," she said, "give it to me, fuck the shit out of me." And with yelp and hammer I was beginning to; with fire and tongs I sat in the saddle, hauling myself through the deep fires underneath, plenty of juice there—fifty-one years old or not—pulling myself slowly up the long mountain; and then the quick slide beginning, around the slick crevice on the bobsled and down toward the chasm, yanking and pulling, riding her like a mountain climber now zooming down the opposite slope; and just at the timorous peak, of course, I heard the slamming and shouts at the door.

"Bill!" Brick was shouting, "Bill, open up in there. What's going on?" And I looked at her, trapped in some cartoon of astonishment, to see that she was already over the edge, pulling, sucking me in, her hands like webs on my shoulder.

"Don't stop," she said, "for God's sake, don't stop," the pounding on the door accelerating. But what was there to do? One cannot displease a lady; a lady's wrath is terrible (I am in a position to know of this) when denied that which has been wrung with such difficulty from them. "Don't stop," she said, increasing her movements; and like a butterfly pinioned in her grasp, I kept on swooping and fluttering, wondering vaguely at the storm-center of the motions if this is how heart attacks were induced in overaged, overexcited men—this would be no way for the campaign to end.

Sucked in, clambering within her, I felt myself suspended between the urgency of the cries outside, the signals of an advancing and demonic press, and the other, more immediate signals from my wife underneath me. Some state of suspension this was, to be sure, on the one hand stay and finish and risk disgrace, discovery, stories which would circulate through the press rooms for years; on the other, seal her up in the midst of her own slow ascension, meaning that similarly for years or at least months afterward I would bear the burden of her anger, Hope being slow to forget anything that ever happened to her. The fact that my own orgasm had not occurred was almost incidental, peripheral to this more immediate issue; at the moment my own satisfaction meant nothing; my own satisfaction indeed would have been my disgrace, because how (I could see her asking), how could I be beast enough to satisfy myself while leaving her suspended!

Oh, my dilemma was awful, and you can understand that I have painfully here, brick by brick, mortar of the most painful substance, constructed a metaphor, a metaphor for all the political dilemmas of our times. The personal or the professional? The incessantly internal or the more generalized demands of those who seize upon us? Are we men or machines, are we devices or artifacts? Do we hunger for the populace's approval because we have no approval of ourselves, or rather is it some eternal self-image which we are trying to dredge out of the circumstances of our struggles over and over again?

Well, I do not know. Although putting the question, as they say, is in itself at least half of the answer; the question can *be* the answer, and I have put it as forcefully as I can, not even altering the facts and difficult circumstances of my life in order to do so. . . . But it was the cunningly planted question of my own averted orgasm which was the solution to this dilemma, because I was failing and failing against her, even as I twitched in her grasp; so I was failing, the diminished flesh falling, and I could not sustain after a short time even the substance of entry. She gave me a look of such disgust that you will never know; I cannot possibly explain that look—it was the first time I had ever seen that expression on her face.

"Go on," she said, "get off, you disgust me." And with some surprising agility, more strength in her thighs than I would have conceived, she tossed me off. I rebounded from the bed nearly falling to the floor, and she as she lurched up from the bed, a rather furious expression on her face, fury clotting all of the arteries, pressing color through all the opping and disintegrating vessels underneath the skin, I understood that her rage in many ways went beyond my own and as was her rage magnified, so was her pain . . . pain at insufficiency, which I had never before understood. Putting it another way, she felt fifty-one to be more terrible than I did seventy.

"You'd better get the door," she said. I was already lumbering toward it, my discombobulated, detumescent little organ bobbling like sacrifice within the urn of my pants. "You want to make all of your appointments," she said. "You wouldn't want to miss anything, after all; we know what's important in this world, don't we?"

That was the last time I think that she ever showed passion in sex; we had a good deal of sex together, but it was automatic, reflexive; feeling seemed to be squeezed out of it. And soon enough I saw the fundamental ridiculousness of a man in his seventies trying to have sex; you can kill yourself doing that kind of thing. It all fell away shortly after Eunice's funeral; it just would have been obscene to have tried to rekindle any of that anyway. That is campaigning. You are here and you are there, but it is always in and out of the same dark corridors until you are spilled free forever.

"I've never been offered a bribe before," I said. "I can't believe your audacity. Go away and I'll make believe that this never happened. Go away and I'll put this out of your mind."

"Don't be a fool, senator," he said, "this isn't a bribe; this is a contribution. Anyway, what do you care? What are you talking about with that law firm—"

"Get out of my office," I said. He was a fat old man and there was no subtlety in him. "Get out of this office right now or I'll turn you in."

He stood—he was quite graceful for all of that bulk—and laughed at me. "You're a fool, senator," he said, "you're a fool because you think that *we're* fools. But you can't get away with this kind of thing forever; sooner or later you're just going to have to face up to what you are. We have. Everybody in the world has got to, and you'll have to do it too. You just don't like the approach," he said laughing, "because you're not sure of your ground. Believe me, I wouldn't be here if it wasn't all right; you know it's all right, senator, don't you?" As I got to my feet, he laughed at me, laughed and laughed. I looked at that face and the face of course was myself; and the dialogue must have been in the sheets at night.

"Eunice," I said, coming out of it, "Eunice, this is ridiculous. I can't take it anymore. Please hold me." And she held me, of course; she always did;

131

she was very good that way. I was never able to separate dreams and reality sufficiently in my mind, but I am glad to say that I kept them straight on the business end of things.

What do you think? he said to me. You think we're a pack of bums? You think this is a two-bit cheap-jack operation? You don't give me that bullshit, buddy, you just come right off it; you're dealing with the top here. When you're dealing with the attorney general of the United States; you're dealing with credibility and power and honor gilt-edged. If you're going to deal with the attorney general you're going to deal with a man who can deliver. We're not asking anything that we can't follow through on. At these kind of prices, we demand and get the best. And frankly I'm appalled at your attitude. You can take your business and money elsewhere if you're going to insult us like that, insult the attorney general like that. What do you think? Don't you realize that you're not dealing with two-bit crooks here, you're talking about the attorney general of the United States, and he delivers.

To say nothing of the commerce secretary.

Bitch, I said to her, although of course I said it silently; there was no need to say it to her face. Bitch, you can't do this to me. You're twenty years younger; you're not going to die. You're going to live past me by at least thirty, you bitch. You knew it; you were counting on it. So was I. How can you tell me you're going to die? First Arthur, then Eunice, now you. I tell you I won't take it anymore. I won't take this horseshit; now tell me you're all right, tell me this is all crap.

Leaning over, thinking this but saying nothing —oh, God, she looked terrible against the pillow, white against a denser white, her eyes bleak, and the doctors saying you've got to get out of here, you can't tire her anymore, she only has so much strength . . . it was inoperable of course, things like that are always inoperable. I knew a good deal about cancer by that time—I should. The face was halfway toward ash now bone, but I could see the fierce, glinting determination in her eyes; talk about not going gentle, she wasn't going gentle, not Hope, she would hold onto herself toward the end; she had always reacted toward illness that way—colds, menopause, viral pneumonia—it was a personal insult, an explosion of the body against the psyche which she simply would not tolerate. That is what she thought, but it was no good—I knew that too. It was impossible to see bravery in it or conviction, metaphor, or strength; it was merely death, that was all.

But this was impossible . . . the woman was fifty-seven years old. People do not die at fifty-seven. I didn't. In my fifty-seventh year, my primary difficulty was in finding an acceptable position on the war issue that would not clash with the positions I had arrived at before, but at the same time would establish that I was moving more to the left. . . . Nothing as personal as death ever got between me and the war issue. How could this be?

I found myself wondering if I gave cancer. I understand that this kind of guilt is often present subconsciously with close relatives of the cancer patient, the fear of contagion turned around and projected into an exaggerated guilt for being the carrier . . . but in my case it was more personal. First Arthur, then Eunice, now Hope, the same disease, even the same symptoms early on—weakness, loss of weight, the enlargement of the eyes in the shrinking skull. . . . Was it possible that I was giving it to them? Clearly I could not be; and yet the common denominator in all three lives was my presence, my kiss planted upon them, my touch, my hope, my closeness. . . . I had fondled Arthur often as a baby, in later years I had not fondled him at all. This would have been abnormal, but could that dark kiss of the cells been then implanted? I did not know. Nothing was to be known.

But thinking about it, being obsessed with the possibility kept me from thinking about more painful and direct things, like how I was going to survive without Hope, how I was for that matter even going to get through the funeral . . . oh, it was too much for me, too much by far; and yet had I not always known at the root that she would die before me? Everybody would die before me; it was with that sublime conviction that I had entered politics, a profession in which advancement is only possible as those senior perish. To be convinced of one's political success is to be convinced only of one's long-delayed mortality. So I must have known it.

Then toward the end I was unable to function at all, weeping around the hospital. The press was into it, of course; there was no way they could be avoided, and my posturing frame was always good for a third- or fourth-page picture on the slow days, although out of discretion they would get me coming or going, chatting busily with "aides"—never pounding the walls or rubbing at my eyes.

And then the obligatory death scene, nicely timed, managed to the absolute, as only Hope could have done it; first the summons from the room where she lay surrounded by equipment and nurses, half-propped on the bed, her eyes brighter than they had ever been before; and at the center of them this deep rage.

"Bill," she said, "Bill, this is the end. I cannot survive this."

"Oh, Hope, you will—"

"No," she said, "this is my decision. I'm going to let it end now. I want to die. I'm ready to die. This is good-bye, Bill."

What a woman! What a scene! The strength of it was incredible. It was hard to believe that the woman could manage it with such finesse, such a powerful control of circumstances. It was only later that I understood that she had only been trying to manipulate factors out of the belief that if she were able to manipulate them right up to the end, she could similarly manipulate away death . . . elect to spring from the bed at the last moment, her last victory of scheduling, and greet me in the corridors. I know the syndrome well, now. I am engaged in it myself. I cannot possibly die until I finish these tapes, the true and real story of my life revealing factors hitherto unknown, passions never unrevealed . . .

But it did not work for Hope, as it will not work for me, as it will not for any of us. She died near dawn the next morning—which is when most of them die, I understand—a willed death too, with the body at the lowest ebb . . . she must have expected that if she carried it through to the end, she would spring through the ceilings for sunrise. But no such thing happened. The news was carried out by messenger, and I received it with no surprise whatsoever, not even surprise that she had not wanted me at her bedside at the end. Hope's gestures were always accomplished best in privacy; she would take her sex straight but with her eyes closed, her limbs opened but her face locked. People take their death in the same manner that they take their sex, and Hope always took hers neat with just a little shot of pain on the side. It was at about that time that I began to feel that great and grievious sense of isolation which, to be sure, has controlled the impulses underlying so many of my later acts.

Here I lie, feet to the ceiling, babbling. The vasal dilators—or whate'er they are called—which Goodenough now administers to me at the rate of three or four a day, the vasal dilators are having a little effect upon me, even I can see this. My thinking seems to be a little more straight-line, a little more lucid . . . although the ponderous depression which has now settled over me as a side effect of the drugs is hardly pleasant. It is not a pleasant thing to see oneself as a worthless, piteous object, but then again this may be not a side effect of the drugs but merely the outcome of my clearer thinking, my new perspective on the situation as aided by the drugs. . . . One can hardly say that my outlook is hopeful. What is there to look forward to? What exactly could be said to be my prospects? But I do not wish to complain. I have never tried to be a complaining sort.

You remind me of my son, Arthur; this is what I should have said to the man in my office. He would have been just about your age, but of course I do not think that he would have been as bitter as you. Arthur had all of the advantages. It was not my fault that he failed to take advantage of them; certainly they were there. And even though there was some profound failure in the boy, some inability to confront possibility, still he would never have hurt people. That is your trouble; you are hurting people—don't you understand that they are not abstractions? That in detonating power plants you are killing people? Don't *people* matter to you, or is it all a question of causes? Well, I did not ask that, and good thing, because the answer surely would have depressed me, out of all proportion to the manageable.

We're trying to save the human race. Shit, he would have said, when you're dealing with the human race what do a few *people* matter?

Hope didn't matter dying—she was already an abstraction, that to be retained in memory, that which I would look back upon at a different time with an entirely firm and certain feeling. She would be objectified in memory. Hurry up and *die*, I was thinking in the hospital; the sooner you die, the sooner I'll be able to remember you with pain and horror, pity and astonishment . . . what the hell good are you to anyone lying in the bed preparing to die? It must have been the same with the man in my office; come on and capitulate so that I can relish. He was not even confronting me. And of course back in the early days with girls, I couldn't wait sometimes for a date to finish, for the petting and necking and fucking to be done so that I could go back to my room and begin to cherish it.

Maybe I should have served in the army; a commission was ready and waiting, it would have been easy. But politicians were exempt, of course, and I was thirty-one years old; besides, I thought I would do the war effort more good by staying in the statehouse and keeping an eye on the profiteers ... sure, I did. This was my rationalization, anyway. And what with a year-old son and a wife who depended on me for everything, what business did I have going into the army? Anyone who says that I saw the war coming and picked up the assembly race to stay out of the draft will be instantly dragged out of here and burned by presidential fiat—oh, yes indeed. You bet.

"I've never had an injection like that," I said. The vial was filled with orange fluid, viscous, deadly orange fluid. "I won't take it."

"Yes, you will," Margaret said, "it's for your own good. It's a palliative. You'll find that it relieves—"

"You're trying to kill me," I said. The insight came upon me suddenly, and all the events of the last week swung into place. Merrick gone; Henry no longer near me at all except for certain vagrant clean-up details; my contacts restricted to Margaret; Goodenough having moved in. I should have seen it from the first. "You want to kill me," I said.

"Honey, don't be ridiculous—"

"Don't call me honey," I said. "I'm the president of the United States, no bitch nurse calls me honey. It's all a plot; you're here to kill me. I know too much and I'm saying too much, and now you want to kill me. You're all spies from the administration."

She hovered near me, the needle in view. The fluid swirled sickeningly like blood in the phial; I imagined that I could smell it. She shook her head. "Look sweetie," she said, "I know you're not feeling too well, it's common; this will make you feel a lot better. We're all here to help you—"

"Help me?" I said. "You're not here to help me, you're the angel of death. You were put on this job to kill me, you and Goodenough worked the whole thing out." I found myself literally babbling with terror. Hoisted up, compressed into the stockings, squeezed like a gnome into helplessness, I saw the terrible needle closing in on me and realized what they had done. Step by step I had been led to this from the moment that Hope had died and they had put me in isolation, then filling me with drugs so that my condition deteriorated, administering deadly, painful drugs to me under the guise that I was ill and that they were curing my illness . . . it was the drugs that were making me sick! "You bitch!" I screamed, thrashing around, trying to rise—but it was hopeless. I was helplessly pinned. "Get away from me. Get away from me with that!"

Her face swung before me, moonlike, enormous, pendulous, that face suspended like a hanging tear from the panel of her forehead. "Mr. President—" she said.

"No!" I said, "no!" and bellowed then so loudly that I must have terrified her; if nothing else, I still have power in my voice, I have the habit of command. A president is still a president, no matter what they do to him, what drugs they fill him with to make him weak. And she backed away from me, the needle shaking. I saw everything. I saw everything then—how cunningly I had been led step by step to exactly this position, what they had done to me, what they were planning to do. "Bitch!" I screamed again and with a mighty effort thrashed free of my confinements. I fell in a half-roll to the floor, the two-foot drop shattering; it was as if every bone within the body took the shock, the muscles spavining; and I lay there then looking at her with hatred.

"You fell," she said. She reached toward me, putting the needle horrifyingly *between her teeth* as she leaned forward like some grotesque animal then, shades of light washing her face.

How I bellowed and thrashed! This next presidential wail must have cut its way through all of the chambers and pockets of 1185. I squirmed like a rodent under this fury, my body literally melding with the floor. I had never had this sensation before, that there was no differentiation between the body and the surfaces on which I slithered—a snake must· feel this way, the crawling and dreadful things in the unseen forest, half creatures of the slime, half of corruption. And winding underneath her that way, everything came into focus as it never had before! I realized that from the very first they had been out to kill me and that they had used my obsession with my memoirs as a means of distracting my attention from their purposes.

"Old cunt!" I screamed, lying there, "I know what you are. I know what you're doing!" And she started to come forward with that needle again; but sly, sly in my weakness, I rolled again.

"You'll get yours," I said, "you'll get yours, all right. I'll put everything down on tape. I have already. I know what you've been trying to do, and I've put down the most explicit details. It's all there for the police."

This was a lie, of course, I had put down no details at all. But it was enough to make her think. I could see connivance and dismay mingle in my eyes, and at that moment Goodenough came into the room.

"What is this?" he said. I could see him looming huge by the doorway. "What is going on here?"

"She's trying to kill me," I said. "She's trying to kill me with that thing. You are too; you've been planning this from the first." If nothing else, I was always very free and frank with my public announcements. There was no duplicity in me at any level; I would always say what was on my mind. After decades of lies, they appreciated me

141

as straight-talking Bill. "You've been planning this from the first," I said.

He knelt by me. His face too was pendulous, but rather than glistening like a tear, it was dull, dull. "Bill," he said, reaching toward me, "Bill, you can't—"

"Don't touch me, you murderer!" I shrieked, pivoting on the floor; but he was after me in a flash, scuttling on hands and knees, and he laid his strong, calm hands on me and yanked me to a halt. "Murderer!" I shouted, "you've touched me!" —and then let my body go limp in his grasp. I would not give him the satisfaction, I would not permit him the satisfaction of weakness or pleading but rather would become completely submissive. I would disappear within his grasp. I felt myself being lifted then, whisked levels and levels, as if in skyscraper by elevator; and with moans and little hisses of effort, I was placed down on the couch again, where I lay at my swooning ease, the cannister tucked into place, again the stockings tightened, my feet hoisted high, high over my head, my head pushed down firmly into the matting. Still I kept my eyes closed; if I kept them closed, there was nothing they could do to me, no way they could reach me—like being young again and under the covers, where no nightmare could get me. "I want you to listen to me," he said, yanking at my hands, pulling at the fingers. "I want you to listen to me now."

"Nothing. I won't listen to you."

"This is very serious now. Your condition is too far advanced. If you don't listen to me, we're going to have to institutionalize right away. I'll call an ambulance. I'll notify the press too, so they'll

142

all be here to take pictures when they carry you out."

That brought me into alertness. Slowly I unsealed my eyes, zipped them open. "Don't even think of that," I said. "I have a right to do as I see fit. I have a right to protect myself."

"Get out of here, Margaret," Goodenough said, "I want to talk to him alone."

"I'll get out of here," she said. "I am leaving this house. I am never coming back. He has accused me of trying to murder him. I don't care if he's the ex-president of the United States. In forty years of practice—"

"Forget it, Margaret," Goodenough said, "I don't want to listen to your nonsense now. Get out of here."

She left, her needle with orange phial still in her hand. Obviously she had forgotten that she was still holding it. I did nothing to remind her.

"Listen to me," Goodenough said when she was out the door, "I think we've carried this as far as possible now. I don't think we can go this way anymore. You're going to have to be institutionalized."

"No," I said. "I know you're trying to kill me," I added. "I know you've always been thinking of it. You had me fooled for a long time, but now I'm onto you."

His eyes flicked, he tapped his knees. "Then you should be happy," he said patiently. "If you think that we're trying to kill you, then obviously you're unsafe here; you'd be better off in a place where you would be watched all of the time, where you wouldn't have to be fearful."

"Fuck off," I said. "It's my life, I can do anything I want with it. I want you out of here with your lousy nurse in an hour, that's what I want."

"I'm sorry," Goodenough said, shaking his head, "if no one can take the responsibility, then it falls to me. I have no choice. I didn't want it to be this way. But the paranoia is starting now. When the paranoid syndrome begins, it means that you're entering an area of potential clot, and if you get a clot, you could bow out . . ."

"What do you mean, paranoia?" I said sullenly. "You mean you're not really planning to kill me, that this is just something I've imagined?"

"Exactly," said Goodenough. "It's a very predictable part of the syndrome, but I hoped that we could avoid—"

"Get out of here," I said. "Murderer! Assassin! I managed to survive the curse, and if I can do that, I can survive you! I won't permit you to have me, even though you've been stalking me since the day I was inaugurated. I cheated you fair and square; you couldn't catch up with me, and you're not going to have me now. You'll have to live with the knowledge of your defeat. Fair's fair; if you couldn't get me when it was open season, then you can't get me now!"

"You don't understand," Goodenough said, "you're a very sick man."

"I'm not that sick. I'm not so sick that I don't know what you're trying to do to me. I'm going to outlive you," I said. "I'm going to outlive all of you. William Eric Springer will live to the age of ninety-five in the year 2005 and will bury all of you."

"I can't be responsible," Goodenough said. "I've done everything within my power to keep you going. But now I'm going to have to call in other parties. I can't take the responsibility alone any-more."

"Don't you threaten me," I said. "I'm not afraid of you."

"It was my responsibility up until now," Good-enough said. He began to move toward the door in sidewise scuttle, his motions awkward and yet somehow graceful in the way that Margaret's had been. These people are clever; they live on levels; it is impossible to see any consistency within them. Only I have been consistent; and up until the ab-solute end, that is how I will remain. Consistent. True to myself.

He stopped at the door, hanging over it like some ghastly ornament. "Will you cooperate?" he said. "This is your last chance."

"How should I cooperate?"

"Follow medical procedures," he said, "follow medical advice. And the dictation will have to stop. It's too dangerous. You're becoming overly excited—"

"I am going to finish my memoirs," I said. "I am going to make my true and final statement. No one can stop me."

"It will kill you," Goodenough said. "You've built yourself up to a peak . . . "

"You've been listening to them. You've been spying on me."

"No one's been listening to you," he said. "No one's been spying on you. You've constructed all of this in your mind. You've created a set of fantasies that cannot be punctured. This is part of the arteriosclerotic pattern."

"Fuck you, you son of a bitch," I said. "Go get laid."

"This is all my fault," Goodenough said
145

vaguely. "I did this. It did not have to be this way. It could have been different."

"Leave me alone."

"I admit that I identified with you. Your struggles to get it all down, to recapitulate your life. It was unprecedented. It was something that had never been done before. I thought it could be a valuable contribution to history. I thought it could be an important part of the historical record. It was vanity. I wanted to share in it vicariously."

My stockings were pinching. "Leave me alone," I said, waving the microphone at him. "I've got everything down on tape, you son of a bitch. Everything that you've been saying, all of your plans and plots. Wait until the courts get hold of this. You'll be jailed for manslaughter."

"I'm sorry," he said, "I'm very sorry." He left the room, leaving the door to sway in the abscess, like a gigantic ear torn from a dismembered body, the breezes from the corridors causing it to twitch to and fro in its vague way, like a misplaced synapse. I felt an assumed control. Holding the microphone, I had the feeling that I had once again taken over some control of my life. They could not get away with this. They would not. All of it was on the record. All of the time, always, they were out to get me, but I was too cunning for them, and even at the end I had the power. I have the tape. I have the memoirs. I have the absolute consistency from first to last of my own position.

"What's a senator, daddy?" Arthur said. "What does a senator do?"

"That's hard to explain," I said. "A senator is a member of the highest legislative body in the United States."

"What's a legislative body?" he asked. He was only nine years old, fourth grade, I had to keep on remembering that.

"A legislative body is a group of men who make and uphold the laws of this country and also represent the opinions of the people."

"All the people?" he said

"The people who elect them," I said, "the people who vote for senators, two from every state. If you get more votes than the person running against you, then you become a senator and it's your duty to act as the people who voted for you would. To let their wishes be known to the whole country."

"Mommy says that this is going to mean you'll be away from home a lot," Arthur said. "I don't want you to be away. You're away too much already. Will you ever be home if you're a senator?"

"Oh, yes," I said. He was always able to get through to me emotionally in a way that Eunice could not; no one could reach me as Arthur did. This may be some betrayal of tragic weakness—I am not looking for sentimental response now, being far beyond that—I really believe that this is a flaw in me that he was able to reach me so deeply on an easy, superficial level of connection, when the fact is, that at the bottom he did not care for me at all, nor I for him; we were merely linked genetically, that was all. "Yes, I'll be home, don't you worry about that."

"No, you won't," he said, "you'll never be at home. You don't like to be at home."

"Who said that?" I asked. "Who said that?"

"I said it myself," he said, and then he turned, ran down the panel of beach, blue bathing trunks against the white of him, against the brown of the sand, the sea coming in. I heaved myself from my back and pursued him slowly, limping, running down that streak of beach after him, out of breath, weak from having risen suddenly, the absolutely first intimation of mortality that must have been at nearly thirty, the realization that not even I was going to live forever. But I wanted to catch up with him, the beach house in the background, the sun falling away over my shoulder as I pursued him; and he waited for me, his run slowing to a lope. I caught up with him, reached out, touched a shoulder, and turned him around.

"You should never say that," I said. "You should never say that I don't want to be home; you should never believe that."

"But it's true," he said, his boy's face bleak, the absence of expression of the imprint of experience upon that face, giving him oddly a sense of greater corruption—as if the maximum corruption, I thought, might be no experience at all, like the smooth and blasted faces of the old in nursing homes.

"It's true, isn't it? You always said to tell the truth in this world, and I am. The truth is that you don't want to be home."

And what could I say? There was nothing to say. I reached toward him, meaning only to comfort him, to stroke his arms, to lift him into the air against me; but he must have taken something in this gesture for threat, for he turned and was running down the beach again, faster this time; he was running in something which could have been real fear, his legs pumping, eyes and head fixated, arms moving steadily and slowly. And as he ran away from me, as I watched him dwindle and diminish, I knew that I should have pursued him. This was something that I definitely should have done; I should not have let him run away alone. But I did not know what to do, did not know what could have been said; and turned instead, let him go away from me, began to walk slowly back toward the house where Eunice was waiting, hands on hips, the sun glinting off her head like glass an explosion of light around her head.

I should have followed him, but I did not; instead I went back to her. Tropism. That was the nature of my life; it was always tropism until the greatest one of all came to take me . . . and then I refused to realize what had happened, and instead called it bad luck.

Politicians.

Even when we have learned, we know no better.

It was only a thousand dead, twelve hundred at the most in the two detonations before the blackmailing demand was made; the next would have escalated, however, and then beyond that, and there was no question in anyone's mind but that at least forty or fifty thousand Americans were being risked by my refusal to negotiate. We would have broken the ring; there were only twenty of them altogether—twenty: Unbelievable. But it would have taken time, and in the meanwhile there would have been forty or fifty thousand dead, maybe much more than that if a chain reaction had been set off by any of the explosions. Later on we realized that this had been a real possibility. But even forty or fifty thousand was considerable; it would have been the greatest national disaster of its type in history, as many dead as in the Vietnam war.

I was asked, as I inevitably would be, at one of the press conferences whether the stakes had ever crossed my mind . . . that is, if I had ever for a moment doubted the wisdom of my actions, if I had not held back from the consequences. This was still early after the incident, when I was running, so to speak, on a floodtide of national approval and sympathy; and if the question were ever to be asked, this was the time to take an honest answer . . . but I found myself astonished to realize at the time that it was being phrased that I had literally never thought of it. I had just never thought of it at all. I had never doubted for a moment that the only way to handle the situation was to deny all demands. Their desires were untenable and were in no sense negotiable; to have capitulated would have brought even greater disaster. It never occurred to me to give in to them. This was the answer, as a matter of fact, that I gave.

"Yes," the reporter said, "yes, I understand that. Would you say this was the same kind of thinking that lay behind Truman's decision to use the atomic bomb? The decision to save more lives by risking some. Or Johnson's decision on Vietnam?"

I had never thought of that either. I did not like the equation between this and Vietnam, and I said so. "Vietnam was a policy misjudgment," I said. "Everybody knows that now. Vietnam was not acceptable risk for the returns."

"And Hiroshima? What would you say about Hiroshima?"

"I don't know," I said honestly. "I just don't know. I was barely in the Congress then. I was thirty-five years old. What part could I play in it?"

"But surely you've given it some thought. I mean, in all the years that have followed, Mr. President, you must have, as all American presidents have done, pondered this and thought what your own response might have been in this situation. Surely you can't tell us that you never thought of it."

"But I didn't," I said, and I was telling the truth. It was not my decision to make and never could have been, and it never occurred to me for a moment to wonder about what I might have done. Every situation is unique and different.

"Then you're not prepared to say that that decision was right."

"What decision? The decision to bomb Hiroshima? That was almost thirty-eight years ago; there's no way that we can go back and consider that situation. No, I won't second-guess another American president. In my own decision, it seemed that I had no options. Anything else would have been worse."

"Even knowing that forty or fifty thousand—"

"Even knowing," I said, furious, "even knowing that," and pointed for the next question. But this kept on revolving in my brain, just the way the bastard, undoubtedly, had meant it to; it was a

151

setup. In the months to follow, I realized that I had never thought of this—the forty or fifty thousand, that is—they simply did not figure into the equation. All that mattered was on a cost-plus-risk basis, and seen that way, I could not lose by challenging him. The other way was intolerable; they would have taken any sign of weakness for fiat to extend the blackmail, and they had twenty, thirty, maybe forty plants (we simply did not know) under their control. How could I risk it? The greatest good for the greatest number, that was the democratic theorem; but I simply had not thought of that forty or fifty thousand that would have gone in the explosions if they had not been the ones to show compassion.

The reason that I had come out of it so well, I understood finally, was not because of myself, but through them. If they had not been incapable of killing on that scale, I would have been a murderer, because *I* was. All of the time I had been—I had been a murderer looking for an occasion. That was all. I was led to see it. It was the same principle that had underlay the Kennedy heroism in Cuba, the Kissinger settlement in Vietnam. The enemy had simply shown more regard for human life than we had. Then *I* had.

Of course, I never discussed any of this with Hope. There are certain things both in and out of this world which cannot possibly be shared.

I do think, though, that this was one of the reasons for the loss of the election; not because the opposition picked up on it—because they did not—but because somewhere in the lurking subconscious of a good proportion of the electorate was the suspicion that their president was a man

152

who would not hesitate to risk any or all of them for principle's sake; and they did not like this.

I could not say that I blamed them.

The ability to convert people into abstractions is given unprecedented assistance by the technological devices of the late twentieth century, but abstract as we will, there is no similar technological means for the alleviation of pain, as—all of the murderous Goodenough's ministration to the contrary—I am now beginning to understand.

"Come on," she said, "fuck me. Even a senator can fuck, can't he? Unless everything I've been reading is true, and the only person you fellows can get off on is yourself." She was a little heavy in the hips, but a good fuck. Banging away at her, I thought that Eunice would somehow understand; this is what is known as statesmanship.

Merrick had the answer; so did Henry. See it all, listen, retain nothing, forget everything; if you don't know that it's happening, then nothing is happening at all; if a gigantic tree falls in a forest and there is no one within miles around to hear the tree, then it makes no sound. Merrick and

Henry know that without understanding there is no pain, without damned knowledge there is no culpability, without insight there is no guilt. I wish I could have been them and downing the pills one, two, three, the neat red-and-white little pills offered me from those open, glinting palms. It was the feeling that I was taking in not only them but the essence of these spirits themselves, the faithful nurses, my comforters and attendants. I was more than their charge; there was a personal interest. But of course they knew nothing. This is the key to survival in the world. I am not so out of it to know nothing.

If there is an afterlife and if that afterlife is contingent upon knowledge, then we are all in a great deal of difficulty, because to live is to plot out time and again all levels of sensation; to live is to deny knowledge, to become a Merrick or Henry (who can make it very well in this stage but may have some problems with the reincarnation). I do not know. I do not know at all.

I used to piss great, heavy streams. I could do it anywhere, anytime, jab it out in a public urinal, do it next to a press photographer, take a piss while standing in the back hall of the convention, waiting to go out and give the acceptance speech; pissing was as natural to me as breathing and a damned sight more pleasant, even sensual in the welling feeling of the bladder and then that quick sighing release. And now, after a lifetime of pissing, after a veritable lifetime of doing it anywhere and anytime I chose and gaining pleasure from it, I am utterly unable to do it at all, unable to exert any control whatsoever. I suppose that there is in a way some justice in this, but in another and more absolute fashion there is not.

Necessary to get it down. *It was not lust* which drove me to Hope—what was that? It meant nothing anywhere in Washington, and for fifty square miles there were women, delightful, available, attractive women, who were as accessible as one's own imagination, and I could have had any of them (in fact, I had a few). It was not that which drove me to Hope, but something rarer, finer, sweeter. I would never have left Eunice if it had not been for this elevation of feeling. Eunice understood and knew exactly what was going on, but she would not have stopped me. She never attempted to. She let me do exactly what I wanted all of the time as long as I kept up appearances. That was the way of Washington marriages in those times (still may be, as far as I know); and in fact that was the way it was with Hope for a while. All of the pressure came from me, not from her; she had no plans other than her column and an interesting life; it could have gone on that way indefinitely ... it was my own decision to leave Eunice, to marry Hope, to take the indefinable risks to career, even with the Stevenson example before me—that poor, tormented fool ... but not lust. Never lust. That was not any consideration at all. I have always been a considerate and thoughtful man, interested in sex, yes, but never lustful. Just fucking, just fucking Hope, getting in and out of her, moving the tool, digging into her waists, her breasts all around me like flowers, fucking the shit out of her. Who am I kidding? Sanctimonious to the end. How much of this has been the truth and how much the same old lies I will never know, impossible to separate, but I have tried—godammit, I have *tried.*

"No," Goodenough says, "no, it will not be necessary to use force or constriction of any type. He will go without any difficulty at all. Isn't that true, Mr. President?"

I am dictating all of this. I am dictating all of this as it happens, my feet falling below me now with the microphone clenched in my hand and the microphone like a flower, my lips like a child's kissing it. Right up to the end, I wll keep on dictating this; they will not get away with it.

"No," I say, "no, I will not come with you." There are two of them, they look like Merrick and Henry in a way, but they are not; they are big, tall, strong men with blank, weak faces, and they make me feel like a child. They make me feel like a child who could cry, because I do not know them. I can only deal with the familiar; I cannot take these shocks anymore, these constant dull shocks. Too much has happened in too little time.

"No," I say again, "I will not go. It is my right not to go. This is my life."

"Mr. President," Goodenough says, kneeling. Sweat is coming out of a hundred crevices on his face, and I can see the dense little hairs growing out of his nose. "Mr. President, please. Bill, please. It will only be for a little while. Don't you see?"

"See what?"

"See the necessity. It will only be for a little while," he says again. "It is highly necessary."

"No," I say, "I do not want to go with you. I refuse to go with you."

"You will," one of the men says. He extends a hand. "You will, right now."

And I see this, I see this now. Truly I see this they mean business and furthermore they always did. They are going to take me out of here; Goodenough is going to assign me to some institution; and there I will spend the last days of my miserable life. Unable to kill me here, he will drag me into one of his sanitariums; and there he and his trained nurses will do the job. "All right," he says, motioning, "go ahead. Take him."

"Wait," I say. "I want to make a final statement."

Goodenough shakes his head. "There's no time for that—"

"Yes there is," I say. "I'll go quietly when you let me finish, but I'm almost done, I just want to wrap the tapes up. You're going to let me finish them, aren't you?" His blazing little eyes look at the cannisters greedily, watch the reels as they loop through the machine. "They're all yours," I say, "my true and final statement. You always knew you were going to get them anyway. Isn't that what you were after from the start? They can make you famous. Well, you can let me finish them."

"Bill," Goodenough says, "you're very sick. The tapes are almost incoherent. It was something that we let you do to keep your spirits in focus but—"

"But nothing," I say. It is shocking to hear this is what Goodenough thinks of the tapes. "They are not incoherent," I say. "They embrace everything. They make every statement. Go out of the room and let me finish."

His eyes become measured and cunning. "You can do it while we're in the room," he says. "There's no need for any of us to leave."

"Yes, there is," I say. "If you let me finish, I'll come quietly, I won't fight at all. But otherwise you'll have to take me out of here screaming." His eyes seem to close in even further, seemingly unconsciously he pats something in his pocket. "You can't give me an injection big enough to knock me out," I say. "You can never shut away the truth, don't you understand that? The truth will come out someday in some form, and then it will be known to the world. How are you going to conceal it?"

"Leave him alone," Goodenough says. If nothing else, he is decisive; he is not an engaging man, but he can, at least occasionally, face the reality of situations and capitulate to them. "Get out of here."

The two men turn and go. In the slump of their shoulders, in their carriage as they leave the room, I can sense relief. They wanted no more part of this than I did; all along they were hoping for a dismissal. They have lived their lives, I think, wildly, their whole lives waiting for some order that would relieve them of all responsibility, cancel out the fact of their lives themselves; and this underlies their submission and their power.

They will do anything. They will literally do anything to be left alone. So would I. From the first.

"Five minutes," says Goodenough, standing at the door. "You have five minutes. No more."

"Five minutes will be enough," I say to him. "Five minutes is more than I would need." He closes the door. I am alone now, dust in the room, splinters of light cutting their fragments like knives through the turning dust, the microphone in my hand and—

What can I say?

Say this: that as the returns drifted in that night, as the first pattern began to make itself felt, Connecticut breaking for the opposition and then that slide down the eastern seaboard, all of the New England states on the line, no comfortable majorities but close in every state, as the Midwest started to come in with its dismal projections, as New York went under and we came into midnight realizing that this election was lost, the first incumbent president in more than half a century to be turned out of office, I looked at Hope, who had been sitting through all of this, her face somehow brighter and brighter as the evening went on, rubbed to sheen, the wedges of her face implacable and said, "Well, it's for the best. It really is for the best. Who needed this anyway?"

I expected her to laugh; she looked back at me with an expression I had never before seen on her face. There must have been twenty jammed in that filthy little room, but in that glance it was as if it was only the two of us, the two of us only who existed in the world.

"Don't tell me it's for the best," she said, "I don't want to listen to your easy explanations as to why this doesn't mean anything at all."

My God she was angry! She was taking the election personally, but not in the way that a good wife might be expected to—feeling things on behalf of her husband, that is—but rather as an affront to *her*, her own reputation.

"What do you care?" she said. "You always wanted to lose anyway; losing gave you definition; it was your purpose and your salvation and your strength. You're happy now."

"What are you talking about?" I said. I was really puzzled and confused, sitting there with pad on my knee, making scratch marks in pencil, only to give the hands a business; that was the only purpose. And now the pad slid off me to the rug. "I don't understand what you're talking about."

"You fool," she said, "you love to lose. That's why you ran in 1980, because of the curse. You thought you'd be killed. That would make you one of the biggest losers. But then, when that wasn't enough for you, when it looked as if you weren't going to be killed, you tried to set up things so that the world would be blown up——"

I was astounded. I had never heard of anything like this before; I felt my bones turning watery with astonishment. Pouring through, fusing together like sealing wax. "What?" I said again. "What are you talking about?"

"Nothing," she said. "I won't discuss it anymore. I'm sorry I started, forget it, I said nothing, nothing at all," and turned her attention back toward the television, where the Far West was starting to pour in—Nevada down the pipe, Wyoming not holding, Utah (which was a safe state) swinging the other way, fifty-eight forty-two, the early returns out of selected California precincts wholly disastrous.

But my mind was far away from that, my attention swinging on a long, elevated loop—was she right? *Did* I want to lose? Did that explain Arthur, Eunice, the election, everything that had happened? Was I indeed merely seeking, all of the time, a disaster so enormous that it would relieve me of responsibility? I found myself thinking of the others in that moment—Nixon and Johnson and Kennedy, the need for self-destruction which had united that famous trinity—and an insight burst upon me like an apple exploding into filaments from gunshot under a hot, white light: maybe the presidency was a search for disaster, the point where self-revulsion and the abstract, idealistic purposes which could conceal the self from self fused together . . . maybe it was that all the time.

"I didn't want to hurt anyone," I said to her then. "That was the important thing, not to hurt anyone."

"It's too late," she said, "it's too late. You're a fool."

"No one," I said again. I meant this; I did not want to hurt anyone. But it was impossible to keep my posture fixated; my attention on the situation had wandered far away. She had opened new territory—the territory was disaster.

I was on a beach with Arthur. He was running from me; I was running toward him, the waves swinging into the shore. I could not catch him, could not even try to catch him; and so after a while I stopped running and began to move slowly back along the shore toward the cabin, the sun collapsing in the sky, realizing that all of my life had been a search for connection *which would not come,* feeling through pain—and that would come only in intervals.

At the beachhouse, Eunice was there; she looked at me. "What are you doing?" she said. "Don't you know it's too late?"

And I said, "Yes, yes, I know it's too late. Everything from now on must be downhill."

This was in 1949 during the Berlin airlift, and it must have been six months after that—no make it seven—that we got our first wind of Korea, the thirty-eighth, the passage into our dreams, the crossing of fire . . . but to understand then, as the century wound down, that there was nothing, absolutely nothing, that could be said to be ours other than the darkness.

EPILOGUE

The New York Times 4/14/90
. . . . Spokesmen added that no effects were re-trieved; the fire which took the life of the Presi-dent having ravaged his apartment beyond repair. At the behest of the President in a will filed many years ago, the remains were cremated and there will be no services . . . day of national mourning will commence at sundown 4/19 but federal offices shall remain open since, the President stated, "Mr. Springer would have wanted our business to con-tinue."

IT'S ALWAYS ACTION WITH

BLADE

HEROIC FANTASY SERIES
by Jeffrey Lord

The continuing saga of a modern man's exploits in the hitherto uncharted realm of worlds beyond our knowledge. Richard Blade is everyman and at the same time, a mighty and intrepid warrior. In the best tradition of America's most popular fictional heroes—giants such as Tarzan, Doc Savage and Conan—

		Title	Book #	Price
_____	#1	THE BRONZE AXE	P201	$ .95
_____	#2	THE JADE WARRIOR	P593	$1.25
_____	#3	JEWEL OF THARN	P203	$ .95
_____	#4	SLAVE OF SARMA	P204	$ .95
_____	#5	LIBERATOR OF JEDD	P205	$ .95
_____	#6	MONSTER OF THE MAZE	P206	$ .95
_____	#7	PEARL OF PATMOS	P767	$1.25
_____	#8	UNDYING WORLD	P208	$ .95
_____	#9	KINGDOM OF ROYTH	P295	$ .95
_____	#10	ICE DRAGON	P768	$1.25
_____	#11	DIMENSION OF DREAMS	P474	$1.25
_____	#12	KING OF ZUNGA	P523	$1.25
_____	#13	THE GOLDEN STEED	P559	$1.25
_____	#14	THE TEMPLES OF AYOCAN	P623	$1.25
_____	#15	THE TOWERS OF MELNON	P688	$1.25
_____	#16	THE CRYSTAL SEAS	P780	$1.25
_____	#17	THE MOUNTAINS OF BREGA	P812	$1.25
_____	#18	WARLORDS OF GAIKON	P822	$1.25
_____	#19	LOOTERS OF THARN	P855	$1.25
_____	#20	GUARDIANS OF THE CORAL THRONE	P881	$1.25

TO ORDER
Please check the space next to the book/s you want, send this order form together with your check or money order, include the price of the book/s and 25¢ for handling and mailing to:
PINNACLE BOOKS, INC. / P.O. Box 4347
Grand Central Station / New York, N.Y. 10017

☐ CHECK HERE IF YOU WANT A FREE CATALOG

I have enclosed $_____ check_____ or money order_____
as payment in full. No C.O.D.'s.

Name_____

Address_____

City_____ State_____ Zip_____
(Please allow time for delivery)   PB-35

A Question of Balance—
perhaps the most important question the
United States will ever answer—perhaps the
last.

?

Conflict between Russia and China is inevitable—
What does the United States do when *both* sides come
for help?
This is

THE CHINESE ULTIMATUM

P974 $1.95

The year is 1977. Russia and China have assembled troops on the
Mongolian border, and are fighting a "limited" war. A reunited
Germany and a bellicose Japanese military state have joined the
battle. The United States must step in, or be considered the enemies
of both. The Chinese have said their last word on the subject—
what will ours be?

"Absolutely gripping, I couldn't put it down."
            —Rowland Evans, syndicated political columnist
"This novel is too incredibly real . . . and damnably possible!"
            —an anonymous State Department official

If you can't find the book at your local bookstore, simply send the
cover price plus 25¢ for shipping and handling to:
PINNACLE BOOKS
275 Madison Avenue, New York, New York 10016

PB-33

THE MANITOU

"Like some mind-gripping drug, it has the
uncanny ability to seize you and hold you
firmly in its clutches from the moment you
begin until you drop the book from your
trembling fingers after you have finally
finished the last page."

—Bernhardt J. Hurwood

Misquamacus—An American Indian sorcerer. In the
seventeenth century he had sworn to wreak a violent
vengeance upon the callous, conquering White Man.
This was just before he died, over four hundred years
ago. Now he has found an abominable way to return—
the perfect birth for his revenge.

Karen Tandy—A slim, delicate, auburn-haired girl with
an impish face. She has a troublesome tumor on the
back of her neck, a tumor that no doctor in New York
City can explain. It seems to be moving, growing, de-
veloping—almost as if it were alive! She is the victim of

THE MANITOU
GRAHAM MASTERTON

A Pinnacle Book
P982 $1.75

If you can't find this book at your local bookstore, simply send
the cover price, plus 25¢ for postage and handling to:

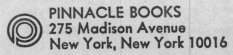

PINNACLE BOOKS
275 Madison Avenue
New York, New York 10016

First there was
THE OMEN
then came
AUDREY ROSE
now there is

The djinn

P40-061 $1.75

Another terrifying page-turner
by Graham Masterton,
author of the best-selling novel,
THE MANITOU
soon to be a major motion picture.

It all begins at the funeral of Max Greaves, a collector of
Middle Eastern antiquities, who has died suddenly, without
warning. His wife is evasive and acts strangely when asked
about Greaves' death. But who is the beautiful young woman
at the funeral and what is her interest in the ancient Arabian
jar Max so carefully locked in the turret room?

The truth about Max Greaves' death is the key to something
more terrible, more frightening, more horrible than anyone
suspects...

If you can't find this book at your local bookstore, simply
send the cover price, plus 25¢ for postage and handling to:

 Pinnacle Books
275 Madison Avenue, New York, New York 10016

An exposé of international financier and
fugitive Robert Vesco... by the man who
served as Vesco's personal pilot and aide

THE FLYING
CARPETBAGGER

by Captain A.L."Ike"Eisenhauer
and Robin Moore
with Robert J.Flood

P985 $1.95

(16-page photo insert section)

"I know things that Vesco knows I know—which worrie
Vesco. I know things that Vesco hopes I don't know—
which worries him even more. And I know things tha
Vesco doesn't know I know—and that really scares the
hell out of him!"   —Captain A. L. Eisenhaue

"...it is a modern adventure story, if you will, the tale
of a jet captain who flew to all points, often with littl
advance notice. The narrative moves along. It's a book
in my estimation, that anyone will enjoy who has eve
been bitten by the romance-of-aviation bug."
            —Robert Sanford, *St. Louis Post-Dispatc*

If you can't find this book at your local bookstore, simply sen
the cover price, plus 25¢ for postage and handling to:

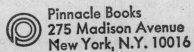

Pinnacle Books
275 Madison Avenue
New York, N.Y. 10016